SOUL DEEP

DIESEL

KING CROW INK
BOOK ONE

MADALYN JUDGE

Diesel
KING CROW INK
TATTOO STUDIO

SOUL DEEP
Madalyn Judge

COPYRIGHT © 2022 MADALYN JUDGE
ALL RIGHTS RESERVED.

No part of this publication may be reproduced in any form without permission in writing from the author.
This book is a work of fiction. Names, characters, places, and incidents either are products of the author's imagination or are used fictitiously. Any resemblance to actual persons, living or dead, events or locales is entirely coincidental.
This content is for mature audiences 18+ only.
Please do not read if sexual situations, violence, and explicit language offend you.

EDITOR: CHASITY MAHALA
PA: CASSANDRA LEIGH
COVER DESIGN: J WAYNE
FORMATTING: MADALYN JUDGE

Hubby,

*I couldn't have done any of this without your support
You always have my back, no matter what I do or what I try and take on.
You're always my biggest cheerleader.
Forever grateful for my very own tattooed badass.*

*XOXO
M.J.*

1

Diesel

"KING CROW INK, DIESEL SPEAKING." The phone has been ringing off the hook today. It's a good thing for business but not great when you're trying to work clients into an already full schedule.

"Dad, you have to do something about mom. She let some guy borrow my PlayStation and didn't even ask me if it was ok. You bought that for my birthday, and she let that loser take off with it." The venom in my son, AJ's voice isn't something that I'm used to hearing. He's talking so fast that I'm not sure what he's said, much less what he's even talking about. This isn't like him at all, he's usually the kid that gets along with everyone and doesn't get his hackles raised easily.

"AJ, slow down, son, and start over. You're talking so fast that I can't keep up, bud." I'm hoping if he calms down he'll be able to focus. It's always hard to understand a word he says because he talks so fast when anyway. I listen as he takes a deep breath and starts over, talking much slower now that he's got his emotions under control.

"Mom has been seeing a new guy named Matt. He's a total loser, Dad. He doesn't even have a car, and he's always borrowing money from mom, even though he has a bunch in his wallet. So why does he need money from her, right? He was here all day yesterday, laying on our couch and eating our food. When I went to bed last night, he was asleep in mom's room with her. I never saw him when I left for school this morning, so I don't know if he was still here or not, but when I got home from school, I couldn't find my PlayStation. I asked mom what she did with it, 'cause sometimes she gets piss—uh, gets mad and puts it in her closet until she ain't mad anymore. When I asked her where it was, she said that she let Matt borrow it. Dad, she can't keep giving our stuff away and she shouldn't be letting people borrow my stuff without asking me if it's ok." I can hear the frustration in his voice but there really isn't much I can do while I am at work. Honestly, when it comes to Charity, there isn't much that I can do, period. The woman doesn't listen to anything I tell her to do.

"Damn. Alright kid. I have a client coming in, in about twenty minutes, but when I'm finished with him, I'll call your momma. Ok?" I ask, hoping it will appease him for the time being because I really don't have time to deal with Charity's shit right now. My blood pressure rises when I think of how selfish she is. I'm really getting fed up with all of her shit. AJ has been asking more frequently about coming to live with me and I'm not sure what to do about that. It may be time to start considering filing for full custody. I haven't done it so far because I'm trying to give her a chance to fix her shit.

"Yes, Sir. She went somewhere with Matt and probably

won't answer her phone when you call, though. I guess I'm going to go down to Mason's house for a while and play his PlayStation with him. Dad, when you talk to her, don't let her tell you any lies because she let Matt take it, and she'll try to lie to you about it," I've been dealing with his mom long enough. I already know to be prepared for that, but I let him warn me, anyway, not wanting to say anything bad about his mother to him. I never want my views of her to taint his.

"All right boy, be good. I'll call you tonight before you go to bed and let you know what your momma has to say. Love you, kid." Crow grins when I flip him off for listening to my conversation like the nosy ass that he is. He smirks before leading his client down the hallway.

"Love you too, Dad." He hangs up without saying "goodbye." I really gotta work with that boy on his phone manners. That's a problem for another day, though. When I place the phone back on the receiver, I look around the shop and realize how far I've come in the last eleven years.

My career is booming and I owe a lot of that to King and Crow for taking a chance on us. My dad and I had been working in a shit hole shop on the other end of town. They had built a bad reputation for themselves and me and my dad. Damon did our best to rebuild the name but there was no coming back from the shit work they'd done in the past. We stayed because the rent was cheap and nobody else in town was hiring. Now we're blessed to be working in the best tattoo shop in the south. Damon and I have been proving ourselves as valuable assets ever since. It took a few years, but I have built my reputation into something that I can be proud of.

My personal life is another matter altogether. I have made so many mistakes which usually involves trusting the wrong people. Like marrying AJ's mother right out of high school, for example. That was a huge mistake. How big of a mistake was proven when I came home and found her in bed with another man while my son was asleep in the next room. It was a shit storm of epic proportions but on the other hand, I wouldn't have AJ without having been married to the woman and he's worth living through a thousand shitty marriages.

AJ had been five at the time I caught her. I wasn't able to control my anger and ended up spending six months in jail for assault, which meant that when our divorce was finalized they granted his mother sole custody. My visitation is scheduled but honestly, she lets me have him whenever I want. It's just that he's been miserable living with her ever since our divorce six years ago. It's always something with that woman, nothing ever makes her happy and AJ usually feels the brunt of her unhappiness.

Through it all, I was able to save enough money back to finally be able to purchase a nice pad a few blocks from the beach. King had known that I'd been looking for a fixer upper and when he told me about the one next door to him being up for sale, I jumped on it. My Pop moved in with me and together we renovated the old coastal, five-bedroom home. Six months later, the house next to us went into foreclosure, and Pop swooped in and grabbed it off the market. It's nice having my dad living close so that AJ gets to spend as much time with his Pop as possible; the kid idolizes the man, that's for damn sure. Before long, almost every member of King Crow Ink had purchased a property on our street. King even bought the bungalow next to him a few months ago to add to his rental property empire. I also like that everyone lives close together because it helps to have extra sets of eyes on my boy when he's running the street with his friends.

Crow is the only one who seems uninterested in owning his own place. He's content living in King's rental up the street from us all. That kind of commitment scares him for some reason. I don't think the man will ever truly grow up.

The bell above the door knocks me from my thoughts as my 10:30 appointment comes through the door. "Blake. What's up, Bro?" Blake has been a client of mine for almost my entire career. He's loyal and you can't put a price tag on that.

"Ready to get this piece on my shoulder outlined, dude. I've been pumped all week about getting this done. My girl's been rolling her at me every time I bring it up. She's tired of hearing me talk about it." Blake laughs about his girl giving him shit, but I've met her and she's solid. The woman worships the ground he walks on, but the look on his face causes me to chuckle.

"All right, Bro. Let's get started, and before you leave, I'll get you scheduled for the shading and coloring appointment. The outline will have to heal, so it will be a few weeks before we can finish it completely" Blake has a new baby at home and likes to schedule his tattoo appointments separately, so he isn't forking out a lot of money in one visit. I give him props for putting his kid first.

Blake gets situated so he's straddling the chair. He throws in his EarPods, cranks up his music, and gets in the zone while I work on this piece for the next two hours. It takes a little more time to outline the detailed piece on the back of his shoulder, but it's going to look kickass when it's done.

After prepping the skin and placing the stencil where he wants it, I put on a pair of gloves and get to work. The hum of my tattoo machine lulls me into a trance where nothing but the art I'm creating penetrates my mind. Time gets away from me and before I realize it, a little over two hours have passed and Blake's outline is complete.

Once I clean up the smeared ink and get a good look at it, I can tell it's going to look awesome when it's finished. I apply a layer of protective ointment and then motion for him to check it out in the mirror.

"It's fucking perfect, dude. I can't wait until we get the whole thing finished. It's going to look badass. You're a beast, dude." He continues to rave about how much he likes the outline. I'm always truly humbled when my clients like the pieces that I create for them.

"All right, Bro. Let's get that shoulder wrapped and then I'll take you up front to check out. We had to let our receptionist go, so you get me behind the counter this time," Our last receptionist was a damn nightmare. She didn't want to come in here and actually work. No, she thought she was going to get some free work done and flirt with every man that came through our doors. That shit wasn't going to work for any of us. We run a professional business around here.

Blake follows me back up front where we schedule his shade and fill for a month from now and after paying, he's on his way. As I'm putting the receipt book back in the drawer, King starts shouting for me, from down the hall.

"Just a sec," I yell back.

"What's up?" I check out the dragon he's coloring in on the huge back piece he's been working on all morning and am blown away. I don't know where he comes up with half the shit he designs but his imagination is insane.

"Can you do me a favor, man? My new tenant is moving in upstairs today and mentioned she had a cabinet that she'd need help to move. I told her I'd come by around 12:30, but I have another hour left on this. I really don't want her trying to do it herself and end up tearing up the fucking floors. The last tenants fucked them up so bad, it cost me two grand to get em' fixed."

"Yeah, I don't have anyone coming in for another hour; I have time. What's her name?"

"Paige, you can't miss her. She's got long auburn hair." The smirk on his face tells me there must be something he isn't sharing since he's got a client in his chair.

"I'll go see if she's ready to do it now." I wave over my shoulder as I head back up front.

Pushing through the front doors, I walk around to the back of the building where the stairs are located for the second-floor apartment. It's been vacant for quite a while; people don't seem to want to live above our shop for some reason.

Just as I turn the corner, a tiny boy with curly brown hair and the brightest blue eyes I've ever seen runs right towards me screaming, "Daddy" at the top of his lungs. Quickly I turn around to see if someone is behind me, but there isn't anyone there. When I swing back around, it's to find him leaping towards me. I scoop him up into my arms just in time so he doesn't land on his face in the gravel. For some reason, this little guy launched himself at me and had expected me to catch him. I'm shocked when he latches onto my neck and squeezes as he gives me one heck of a bear hug. When he finally pulls back, he sporting the biggest grin and I feel something in my chest shift at this little guy looking at me with such genuine happiness at seeing me.

Looking away from the smiling boy, I come face to face with a goddess standing before me. Taking in her features and the look of shock on her face, she must be this little guy's mother. She has an identical set of striking blue eyes.

Jesus, this woman is hands down the most beautiful woman I have ever laid my eyes on. She's on the taller side for a woman. Probably 5'10, with legs that go on for miles, long and lean. She's slim with an hourglass figure and a mane of thick brown hair that looks like it's been highlighted from time spent in the sun. Her lips are full and pink and I have an unexplainable urge to know how they taste. There's something about the purple tank top and the cutoff denim shorts with matching purple chucks that are doing it for me. I'm unable to turn my eyes away from her and it hits me like a sledgehammer that she probably belongs to someone. Darting my eyes down to her hand, I sigh in relief when there's no ring decorating her tiny finger.

"Oh my god! I am so sorry! Luke, come here baby, you can't go running off to strangers like that, honey." In the sweetest voice which admittedly sounds exhausted and a smile on her face, she scolds the little guy in my arms.

A miniature version of this beauty glides up right behind her, and I mean glides. This little girl moves with the smooth grace of grown women who walk runways for a living. I can barely contain the laughter when she opens her mouth and that pageant-ready vibe completely disappears.

"Momma, there's a dead squirrel over there."

"Well, leave it alone, Sophia. We don't mess with dead animals."

"He wasn't an 'IT' momma. He was a boy," she huffs, crossing her arms over her chest.

"How can you tell it was a boy?" I'm genuinely curious how this little girl, who can't be more than five or six years old, can tell if the squirrel is a boy or a girl.

"Boys are stupid. He fell out of that tree, so he has to be a boy." She tells me deadpan; with the most serious and straight face that I've ever seen come from a child. Throwing my head back, I roar with laughter. Of course, now it all makes perfect sense. Most little girls think boys are stupid at her age.

"Good grief Sophia! Will you stop with the sass already?" Her mother seems calm but exasperated as she attempts to reprimand her mini-me.

"Sorry. We didn't break loose from the looney bin, I swear. I'm Bella Cruze. This is Sophia, and that little guy who seems to have claimed you is Luke."

"Luke, he's not your father," she says in her impression of a Darth Vader voice, making me chuckle at her attempt at being funny. At least I know she isn't completely perfect. Her jokes are terrible.

"Nice to meet you, Bella. I'm Alex, but everyone calls me Diesel. I work with Max," I tell her, nodding my head towards the shop, unable to stop checking her out. Fuck me, the woman is sexy.

2

Bella

Closing the cabinet door, I look around the kitchen to see if there's anything else lying around that I can put away for Paige. My cousin found this cute little apartment above King Crow Ink and I've been helping her unpack and get things situated before I have to leave for work this evening. For the last year, she lived with me and the kids in the house I had shared with my now ex-husband. It took a while but the house has finally sold and we're set to close soon.

Paige is a hustler and has been working her ass off to put herself through law school and make her dreams come true. I'm so proud of everything that she's doing and all that she's been willing to sacrifice. Things are starting to turn around now that she's almost done with school and getting closer to graduating. This place is perfect for her. She has plenty of room to spread out and a spectacular view of the beach from the balcony. Not bad for a single, twenty-four year old. Especially since it's her first apartment.

Finding nothing else to do in here, I peek into the living

room at the kids who are popping bubble wrap and make my way back into Paige's master bedroom. "Paige, I finished putting all of your dishes and cookware away; what do you need me to do now, sweetie?"

"Do you think you could go wait outside for my landlord? Then bring him up and show him Papa's antique China cabinet that's in the living room. He's supposed to move it into the kitchen for me today. I was afraid if I tried to do it myself, I would scratch the floors. I figured if I asked him to do it, it'll on him if he scratches the floors and not me," she laughs. I can see the logic in that.

"Yep, I sure can. I'll take the kids outside with me and let them run off some of their energy. Maybe Sophia won't keep complaining about being bored if she tires herself out," I tell her. I hope that going outside will distract Sophia, but I seriously doubt there is anything that can brighten her mood. My ex-husband, Trevor, was supposed to have the kids this weekend, but of course, he bailed on them once again. Trevor doesn't care if Sophia is heartbroken that she isn't getting to go to the water park like he'd been promising all week. He only thinks about himself. He's always been like that. I just never noticed it until we separated. It's not a new personality flaw. I have to take some of the blame for his shitty parenting because I allowed him to be this way by putting up with his crap for years. Now he just expects everyone to take whatever he dishes out. The bastard has about pushed me too far. It's one thing to have never kept his promises to me when we were married, but to do this to our children is inexcusable. I wish my children had a better father but there's nothing I can do about it. I can't change the past, no matter how much I wish I could.

Moving back up the hallway, I holler into the living room, "come on guys, let's go downstairs and see if we can spot the squirrels that were running up the tree when we pulled in earlier." I can't help but grin when I hear the sounds of my children's feet on the hardwood floors as they race into the kitchen. I don't know what Sophia's sudden fascination with squirrels is all about, but she loves to lie in the grass in our backyard, and just stare up into the trees, watching them run and jump through the tree limbs above her.

Holding Sophia and Luke's hands, I help them carefully navigate down the steps. Once we hit the bottom step, Luke's little legs work hard to keep up with his sister as she races towards the only tree behind the building. Sitting down on the bottom step, I just watch as my kids laugh and zoom around the base of the tree. The sound of happiness coming from my babies is something I live for.

With a sigh, I think about how different our lives have become. I met their father during my freshman year of high school and we were the 'it' couple that everyone swore would survive the test of time. Well, that clearly didn't pan out. Trevor and I got married right after we graduated and during our sophomore year in college, we found out we were pregnant with Sophia.

Sophia Grace was a blessing to our lives. But it was extremely hard working my way through college while pregnant. It was even harder when that infant became a toddler before I knew it. Trevor wasn't much help either. To be fair though, when he wasn't in class he was working, trying to make life easier for us financially. We knew our hard work and sacrifice would pay off in the end, but like all great things in life, there usually is a struggle too. And struggle, we did.

We were so proud of everything we had accomplished. Especially when we finally made it through to graduation. Our dreams were coming true; I got a job at Mercy General in the ER, where I had always wanted to be, and Trevor was hired at Gulfport High School. We bought our dream home the following year, and everything was going to plan; we were happy. I could never have imagined how far off the mark I had actually been.

It was as we were approaching Sophia's third birthday that I started noticing changes in Trevor. I was working full-time at the hospital and he was working at his dream job at the high school as their Physical Education instructor and had just been made assistant coach of the football team. While he seemed happy with everything that he had accomplished at work, our home life was a different story altogether. Trevor started pulling away from Sophia and me, and I wasn't sure how to fix the divide that seemed to grow a little more every day.

He wasn't interested in hanging out with his wife and daughter when we were all home together. Trevor would leave the house without saying a word to me about where he was going. God only knows what he was doing since he didn't come home until after we were already in bed. I didn't question where he was; I didn't want to be the nagging wife who kept tabs on her husband. Looking back now, I should have, because giving him my trust ended up being my biggest mistake.

After Sophia's birthday things seemed to change again. Only they seemed like they were turning around for the better, or so I had thought. My husband, who hadn't been interested in having sex for months, was once again attracted to me and he was sticking around the house a little more. A few weeks went by before he broached the subject of trying for another baby. I wasn't sure how I felt about adding another child to our family. I was working a lot of hours at the time so that we could afford the life we had grown accustomed to, and I hadn't yet forgotten how hard it had been doing most of the work with Sophia. I didn't think that I wanted to sign up for that again. However, as it always seemed to go with Trevor, he wore me down to the idea of us becoming parents for a second time. Eleven months later, Lucas Myles was born. My baby boy came into this world quietly and has been a soft-hearted soul ever since.

As I had expected, Trevor didn't offer any help taking care of Luke. Right before he left us and filed for divorce, he confessed that he thought another baby would fix our marriage. If I had known he was that unhappy, I could have told him how stupid that idea was. I guess I was in denial that we were as far gone as we apparently were.

It later came to light that all the nights that Trevor had left us, he had been sneaking away to see the woman that he is now dating. Michelle is a co-worker of his at the high school, and it was easy to fall out of love with your wife when you were spending your days chasing after the woman who was readily available.

I eventually had to face the reality that the only man I had ever loved and ever been with, betrayed me by having an affair. He threw away our family like we never meant a thing to him. It turns out the Trevor that I thought I knew had been gone a long time. It didn't end there, unfortunately. The entire time he'd been cheating, he had also been ruining our credit. He put us so far in debt that we had to sell our house to pay off everything he's financed.

"Daddy," my son screams, effectively stopping me from torturing myself anymore with all the what-ifs and awful memories of how far I've fallen. When I look up, I lay eyes on a flipping giant. The man has to be six and a half feet tall and is built like a freaking Mack Truck.

He's dressed in worn black boots, dark denim jeans, and a black T-shirt with the logo *King Crow Ink* sprawled across the front. The way it hugs his muscular body like a second skin is sexy as hell. The giant has a short beard that is meticulously groomed around his strong jaw and his nose is slightly crooked, indicating he's broken it at some point. I clench my fists to physically stop myself from asking him how. As a nurse, I always wonder how people got their injuries.

Watching how he's looking at my son gives me pause. They say that the eyes are the windows to the soul and they reflect a gentle nature. His complete focus is trained on my son's smiling face, which is aimed right back at him. I stand from my spot on the steps and slowly approached them. When he looks up, giving me a better view of the eyes I'm fawning over, I gasp at the sea foam green color. He's devastatingly handsome and his stare is intense as he takes me in from top to bottom.

This man is beautiful and the vibe coming off him is quite profound, but it's calming and gentle. Which completely contradicts his size. He hasn't even opened his mouth, and I already know this guy is a teddy bear in a grizzly's body.

I start to feel worse about everything my ex has put my kids through. Jesus, my poor baby has resorted to assaulting strangers because he's so desperate for male attention. Dammit, Trevor. Then it hits me, this guy is here to move the cabinet and here we are holding him up.

"Oh my god, I am so sorry! Luke, come here baby, you can't run off to strangers like that, honey." As the words leave my mouth, I cringe because even I can hear how tired I sound. Looking down, I try to remember what I'm wearing and realize I look like a beach bum while this guy looks like my wildest dreams. Heaven help me.

Get it together Bella, and stop drooling over the tall drink of water. The man is probably ready to look for the nearest escape route from the asylum he walked into.

"Momma, there's a dead squirrel over there," Sophia says as she comes up behind me and starts tugging on my tank. Leave it to Sophia and her quirkiness to make it even more awkward.

"Well, leave it alone, Soph. We don't mess with dead animals," I tell her as I make sure she isn't carrying it around because God knows she does some strange stuff sometimes.

"He wasn't an 'IT' momma. He was a boy." I don't even want to know why she thinks that, but clearly the big man has different ideas.

"How can you tell it was a boy?" he asks. Oh buddy, you're going to wish you hadn't of asked that in about 2.5 seconds.

"Boys are stupid. He fell out of that tree, so he has to be a boy," she tells him, making him laugh loudly and I realize she was clearly listening to my phone call with Stacie about how men are stupid and would die without women taking care of them. In my defense, we were talking about a patient who was being an idiot about his post-op care.

"Good grief Sophia, will you stop with the sass already?" I swear my baby girl spits out the sassiest comments and just keeps on trucking like she didn't just say the most random and crazy things. I used to laugh hysterically at the things that would come out of her mouth, but I'm so used to her unique brand of zaniness that she doesn't even phase me anymore.

"Sorry! We didn't break loose from the looney bin, I swear. Where are my manners? I'm Bella Cruze. This is Sophia, and the little guy who has claimed you is Luke," I tell him, feeling awkward that my son is refusing to let him go, my daughter has pointed out the local dead animals, and here I stand as the ringleader of the circus. I wouldn't blame him if he ran for his life, leaving us to move the China cabinet on our own.

"Luke, he's not your father," I say referencing the *Star Wars* movie by imitating Darth Vader. Almost failing at suppressing my laughter. You're not supposed to laugh at your own jokes, or so I've been told.

"It's nice to meet you guys. I'm Alex, but everyone calls me Diesel. I work with Max," he says while chuckling at my idiocy as he nods his head back toward the tattoo shop. His voice is as smooth as Tennessee Whiskey and good heavens, is it deep.

"Please excuse me, I'm coming off three back-to-back

12-hour shifts, and I'm beyond exhausted. I swear we're normal and don't usually act like this."

"You're fine, babe. It's cute actually," he says with a grin, clearly not phased at all by us. "So, where is this cabinet that needs to be moved?"

Cute? I don't think anyone has ever thought our insanity is cute. Maybe there is something wrong with this guy after all. He should want to run for the hills after having Luke call him Daddy and cling to him like a spider monkey. Not to mention Sophia talking about dead animals like it's just another Tuesday tea-time conversation. Maybe he's the one who's escaped from the asylum.

"Follow me. It's in the living room," I tell him as I grab Sophia's hand and lead the way back into the apartment so he can move the cabinet for Paige. We've held the poor man up long enough.

3

Diesel

Looking down at my phone, I see Charity should be here any minute with AJ. I go outside to wait for them to arrive because I need to talk to her about this Matt character. If the things I've been hearing around town are true, he doesn't need to be around our son.

It's not long before Charity pulls into the parking lot in her beat-up Honda. She's had the damn thing way too long and should really think about getting rid of it. The car has definitely seen better days and it's a wonder the thing even still runs as hard as she is on vehicles.

No soon does she put the car in park when AJ jumps out like his ass is on fire and storms past me into the building. Guess he and his mom are fighting again. I push off the brick wall I'm leaning on and walk over as she rolls the window down.

"What's he pissed off about?" I ask her as I look her over. She used to be such a beautiful woman, but the years that we've been divorced have not been kind to her. Sure, she's dressed well but everything else about her has declined. Her blonde hair which used to be full and shiny is now dull and stringy. She has dark circles under her eyes like she hasn't slept in days, and she looks unkept which was never her style.

"He's still mad that I let Matt borrow his game thingy. I told him I would get it back, but he's being a brat as usual. I told him I would get it back but he has to give me a few days," she replies nonchalantly, rolling her eyes.

"He isn't being a brat, Charity. You took his shit. That wasn't yours to loan out and let someone take off with it. You'd be pissed off too if your stuff went missing without your knowledge," I tell her while trying to keep my temper in check.

"Whatever, you baby him too much," she says, waving me off.

"We need to talk about this Matt Alvarez you've been seeing. I don't like the things that I'm hearing about him and I don't want him around AJ anymore. People are saying he sells drugs and not just a little weed here and there. He's into some heavy shit, Charity. That isn't the shit you bring around your eleven year old son."

"Those are just rumors. You don't know him and you can't tell me what to do with my son," she hisses, getting pissed off.

"He's my son too and I damn well will have a say in who's around him. Especially if they're into some sketchy shit like this guy seems to be involved in."

"Whatever, Diesel. Do you have my child support or what? I need to get out of here. I have shit to do," she sneers, getting bitchier. I don't care if it pisses her off. I get a say about what goes on in my kid's life too. That's the thing about Charity, she knows that I'm right but she doesn't like being told what to do. It's a game of control with her. It always has been. I just didn't see it when I was trying to do right by my son and married her ass.

"Yeah. Here," I say, handing her the check that I'm court-ordered to give her every week. No doubt that she'll be broke before AJ makes it home on Sunday. I don't know what she does with the child support, but I don't think she uses it for AJ. I'm the one who buys all his clothes, takes care of all his medical care, and gets him everything he needs for school.

Her parents pay her rent. Unless she uses it all on their utilities and groceries, which I doubt she does, I have no clue what she spends it on.

"See you on Sunday when you bring him home," she tells me as she puts her car into reverse and backs out of KCI. Taking off to do God only knows what.

I really need to do something about AJ's living situation. Shaking it off, I make my way back inside the shop to see what my boy wants to get into this weekend.

As I look at AJ, he's the spitting image of me at that age other than the sandy blonde hair that he got from his mother. Everything else though he gets from me. Right now he's tall and lanky. He's been talking about wanting to bulk up, but he isn't anywhere near ready for that yet at only eleven. I was the same way at his age. He has the potential to grow into a big guy like his Pop and me. I didn't bulk up until I hit high school and I wanted to impress girls. I worked out the whole summer before my freshman year, and on the first day of school, I looked like a completely different kid than I had when I finished middle school. That was how I ended up gaining the attention of his mother. I don't know what I did to deserve this kid, but I count my blessings every day that he's mine.

"Where are ya'll going for dinner? I'm getting hungry," dad asks, turning his head towards AJ and waiting for him to pick somewhere for us to go.

"I don't know. What sounds good to you, Pop?" I'm hoping he'll have better luck coming up with something because we don't seem to be making much progress here. We've been sitting on this couch for the last half hour debating what we want and still haven't come up with a single thing that sounds good. This seems like a common occurrence for us. Every other Friday evening we sit here in KCI's reception and go back and forth about what we should have for supper.

"We could go down to The Marina and have Surf-n-turf," dad suggests. I already know this will not fly with AJ. My dad always wants the same thing from the same place. It never fails and honestly, we are burnt out on surf-n-turf at this point.

"Nooo. Not that again!" AJ groans. He's annoyed that his Pop would even suggest eating at The Marina again.

"Well, I'm out then. That's where I'm going. Maybe I can get that redhead to wait on me again. She's hot and I think she has a thing for me," he tells us while waggling his brows suggestively. We both gag dramatically as he stands and leaves without even acknowledging our disgust.

"Gross," AJ says, exaggerating how disgusted he is. He's

in that stage where girls are gross and nothing about them is appealing. That'll change one day. But for now, I'm perfectly fine with him being uninterested in the opposite sex.

"What about pizza, Dad? We could go down to The Pizza Palace. I heard they have a new racing game in the arcade that's supposed to be cool. Teddy said he has the highest score and I want to see if I can beat it." I'm wondering if he thinks of anything other than video games these days.

"All right, that's probably as good as anything else we might have come up with, I guess." I'm not really in the mood for pizza but since I don't have any other ideas, I guess I'll take him so he can try to beat Teddy's high score. I'm pretty sure the kid doesn't care about eating pizza. It's all about the game.

We both climb from the couch we've been lazing on and make our way out into the parking lot where my Harley's parked under a tree in the shade. Reaching into my saddle bag, I grab his helmet and hand it to him. Once he's put it on, I make sure his chin strap is secure and put my own on. I honestly hate wearing it, but I made a promise a couple of years ago to AJ that I wouldn't ride without it. I've kept my word. Better to lead by example because I always want him to wear his.

AJ hops on behind me and wraps his arms around my waist. Pulling my visor down, I slowly inch out of the parking lot and into traffic. It takes us ten minutes to make our way down the boulevard to the east side of town where the restaurant is located. Shutting the bike off, I help AJ off and we stash our lids before making our way inside.

"Dad, this place is packed. What if we can't get a table?" AJ's already getting bummed at

the potential of having to wait a while for a seat.

"Welcome to Pizza Palace. Are you with one of the birthday parties?" The hostess asks us with false cheer.

"No Ma'am. We need a table for two if you have one available." She seems a little flustered from the chaos that's happening all around us. There are kids everywhere and most of them are running around screaming. At least they seem to be enjoying themselves.

"It's going to be a 45-minute wait on a table. As you can see, it's a little busy in here tonight." A little? It's a lot busy tonight. Right as I look at AJ to see if he wants to wait, I hear a familiar voice screaming at the top of his lungs.

Luke, the little boy that I met earlier this week, is yelling "Daddy, Daddy, Daddy," from across the dining room. He's desperately trying to get my attention and Bella is doing her damnedest to calm her boy down. She's gaining quite a bit of attention for her troubles and looks like she's getting embarrassed too, but I honestly don't know why. The boy is cute and nobody seems like they're annoyed.

"Who is that, Dad?" AJ asks me.

"They're the family of the lady that moved in above the shop. I met 'em Saturday when I went to move a piece of furniture for the lady renting the place." At my explanation, AJ walks towards their table and I follow in his wake. Maybe we can help calm the little guy down.

As soon as we got to the table, Luke wrestles his way across Bella's body in his haste to get to me. Seriously, this kid is really something else. I don't know what it is about me, but he really seems to like me and oddly has me confused with his father. Maybe his dad looks similar to me, which seems unlikely because I am such a big guy. There are plenty of muscular dudes running around Gulfport, but not many, are also six-five.

"Hey, guys. We thought we'd come over and see if we could help settle this guy down for you," I say as Luke climbs onto the tabletop and leaps into my arms.

"I am so sorry, Diesel. I don't know what it is about you, but he obviously likes you," Bella tells me apologetically and something about my name falling from her lips has my dick perking up in appreciation.

"Don't apologize, Babe. I'm truly flattered the kid likes me. My size usually intimidates people if I'm being completely honest."

Sophia looks up from her tablet and has me booming in laughter as she says in a rather bored voice, "you shouldn't wear the same tattoos every day. People will think you're poor. That's what my momma tells me when I want to wear my unicorn shirt every day to school."

"Is that right? I'll have to see what I can do about that." I don't really know how else to reply to that. I don't think she will understand the concept of tattoos and most parents don't want their little kids getting any ideas about them either.

When I turn back to Bella she has her hands covering her face as she shakes her head back and forth. Once again exasperated by her daughter's quick wit. This girl could be one hell of a poker player if her delivery of subtle insults is anything to go by. I'm a little shocked that I like these kids as much as I do. Other people's kids usually annoy me, but hers don't.

"Dad, can we sit with them?" AJ asks as he tries to peek over Sophia's shoulder to see what she's doing. I'm about to tell him no and hand Bella back her boy when she waves her hand, indicating that we are welcome to take a seat at their table.

"You sure, babe? We don't want to interrupt your dinner." I really need to talk to AJ about inviting himself to have dinner with people. He's a kid and doesn't understand that it's rude to put people on the spot like that.

"You've tamed the savage beast. I couldn't possibly turn you away after getting him to calm down. Again, I'm truly sorry he keeps doing this to you. Your wife is going to wonder about your secret family if I don't figure out a way to get him to stop doing this when he sees you," she teases, smiling mischievously.

"Dad's divorced," AJ says helpfully as we both slide into the booth with Bella and her brood.

"This is my son AJ," I tell both girls as I place Luke between me and his mother. He relaxes now that I am sitting in the booth with him. Bella smiles up at me and I feel that twinge in my chest again. Something about having her aim the soft look at me feels magnetic.

"So is my momma. My daddy was sticking it to the homewrecker and left us. Momma yelled at me not to be a snoop when she was on the phone. I don't remember what else she said when she quit yelling at me. I wasn't listening anymore," Sophia tells the table and I try hard not to laugh because she has clearly struck a sore spot with her mom.

AJ thankfully hasn't heard what she said, paying more attention to what Sophia is doing on her screen than to anything going on around him, or else he would comment that his mother had done the same thing.

"Oh my god. Shoot me now," Bella says under her breath before letting out a deep sigh. "Sophia, Momma shouldn't have said that. I messed up and I'm sorry you heard it." She genuinely seems upset that her little girl caught her saying what is probably the truth about their father.

"It's ok. Can I have some quarters?" And just like that, she's moving on.

4

♥ Bella ♥

HOURS EARLIER

"Trevor, you can't do this to them again. Sophia has been talking about going with you all week since you made promises to her about all the things you were going to take her to do. It's really crappy to keep blowing them off at the last minute."

"I forgot I had made other plans, Bella. She'll be fine. We'll go next weekend instead." This man is the worst. Does he even love his kids at all?

"She won't be fine. You're teaching them they can't trust you, and that it's ok to lie and break promises. When they get to a point where they believe nothing you say, or they start lying to you, you're only going to have yourself to blame," I say exasperatedly.

"Stop being such a bitch, Bella. This was a big part of the problem when we were married. You never wanted to do anything outside of the kids," he yells at me.

"They're our children! They are our responsibility. You

don't get to pawn your kids off every time you want to run off and be selfish, you jerk!" Ugh! He makes me so mad at how he only thinks about himself.

"Get over yourself, Bella. Tell the kids I'll see them next weekend," he says before quickly hanging up, ensuring he has the last word like he always does.

Sophia is going to be crushed that she will not get to go to the aquarium, and once again, it's going to be up to me to make things right with them. This is how it has always been, even before we divorced. He's always been an absent father, even when he was living with us. Why would it be any different now? These kids deserve so much better than him. They deserve a dad who wants to spend time with them. Someone other than me to teach them how to ride a bike, take them fishing, and how to throw the perfect spiral. Instead, they get the dad that makes promises but never follows through. The one who makes every excuse in the book to avoid talking to them. Trevor couldn't care less and my heart breaks for them every time he disappoints them.

"Hey Soph," I yell down the hallway towards her bedroom.

"Huh?" she yells back, peeking her head around her bedroom doorway.

"Your Daddy had something come up, and he had to reschedule. You and Luke are going to be with me this weekend. What would you like to do tonight, kiddo?"

"Aww, that's no fair. He didn't come last time and promised he would this time." This is exactly what I knew would happen. She's realizing that he flakes on them. If that bastard starts making my baby girl think that it's her fault he doesn't come around, I don't know what I'll do. I never want them to feel like that. I wish there was some way to explain and make her understand that this all has nothing to do with her.

"Well, that's ok. We are going to have a lot of fun this weekend. How about we go over to the Pizza Palace for dinner and then we'll go see the dinosaur movie at the car movies like you've been wanting to do?" She has called the drive-in movies the car movies since she first could talk about the place. It's cute because technically she's right because we watch them while sprawled out on a blowup mattress outside of the car.

"Yeah! That will be fun!" she says excitedly. Thankfully I don't think anything can keep her spirits down for long.

"Lukie! We're gonna go to the car movies and to eat pizza," she shouts as she races down the hall to her brother's room. He's been playing on the floor with his Hot Wheels all morning. He doesn't understand what she's talking about, but he usually picks up on her moods and gets excited because she is. I love how good she is with her little brother. Looks like we're having dinner and a movie date tonight.

Dear lord. Sophia sure knows how to put my foot in it. I apologize once again to her for what I said about her daddy. She should never have heard me say that. I really don't want to say bad things about their father in front of them. They're entitled to love him however they choose. Even if he doesn't deserve it most of the time.

When she asks for quarters, I'm honestly glad she is

willing to let it go and refocus her attention on something else. She's been sad all afternoon, so Diesel and his son are a welcome distraction. Her father bailing on their plans again had her really upset at first, but I'm fairly sure she's already over it. She's going to be an evil mastermind someday and take over the world with her manipulation techniques. I don't have the heart to call her on it, so I am bowing to the whims of my five-year-old tyrant. Whatever. There are worse things she could be doing.

Digging through my big momma bag, I pull out two Ziplock snack bags full of quarters. With working at the hospital, vending machines are a way of life for me, so I always have quarters in my purse.

"Here you go, AJ. Here are some quarters for you too," I tell the handsome boy who looks to be around ten. He is the spitting image of his dad. It's undeniable who they are to each other.

"Sophia, here's your bag, but you have to promise not to make anyone cry in the game room. Share and give other kids a turn. And DO NOT call anyone ugly names. You hear me?!" I warn her as I hand her the bag of coins. Sophia is notorious for being a little shit when she's trying to get her way. Diesel chuckles at my demand for her to behave, but he doesn't have a clue what my girl is actually capable of. She may look like a little angel but she has a mean streak a mile wide.

When the kids take off for the arcade room I'm left alone with Diesel and Luke, and I suddenly feel nervous without the buffer of our children.

"I have to tell you. Your daughter is fucking awesome. I have never in my life seen such a tiny little girl, who looks so sweet and innocent, throw out insults with such finesse it almost goes right over my head," he tells me. He tries to contain his laughter having clearly noticed how Sophia operates.

"I have to admit, I have no clue where she gets it from because it isn't from her father or me."

"So, their dad? Sticking it to the homewrecker?" he says with a grin. He's trying desperately to hide it but I get it. It's hard not to find the humor in hearing that come out of the mouth of my little girl.

When I really look at Diesel I can see his genuine curiosity. With a deep sigh, I unload everything that has happened. I don't know why, but something tells me he just may understand. I must have needed someone to vent to because by the time I finish I've told him everything that Trevor has put us through.

"You're better off without someone who doesn't appreciate the amazing mother and woman you are, Bella. You're a beautiful woman and shouldn't have been treated the way he treated you. It's bullshit you were left to handle everything with your kids all alone, babe." He surprises me with his comment and then again when he tells me how his own marriage ended.

I'm really shocked that any woman would step out on a man as good-looking as him. I tell him that, making him grin at my brazen comment. I'm not typically this forward, but I feel like I can let my guard down with him. As we spend the next half hour talking about our jobs and kids, I can't find a single flaw with the man. Diesel seems like a really great dad that always does what's best for his son. He's also a very successful tattoo artist and has built a pretty big name for himself. I tell him all about working in the ER and some of the weird stuff I see. Without breaking patient confidentiality, of course.

We both laugh and seem to relax after getting more familiar with each other. It's comfortable and admittedly, I am growing more and more attracted to this seemingly perfect man who has yet to stop interacting with my son.

Our server finally makes her way back after tending to her other tables. We order a couple of pizzas and a pitcher of soda so she doesn't have to keep running back and forth checking on us. This place is a mad house and she has her hands full.

Twenty minutes later, our kids return to the table just as our food is brought out. They must have run out of coins for the games. As they're sliding into the booth, AJ asks his dad if they can go with us to the drive-in movie.

"You guys are more than welcome to tag along if you don't already have plans for the night. We are going to the double feature. Soph has been dying to see that new movie about the dinosaur theme park. Luke doesn't exactly cooperate inside a regular theatre. It's too dark for him," I tell Diesel, who is looking at his son with a raised brow in warning. If he's anything like I usually am with Soph, he doesn't want his kid to invite himself.

Ignoring his dad, he continues begging to come along. I really don't mind if they come with us. It's been nice having another adult around to talk to. I'm usually trying to juggle these two by myself and a helping hand has actually been really nice. Unfamiliar, but really nice.

"Are you sure, babe? You guys obviously already had plans, and I don't want us intruding on your family time.

We have already crashed your dinner," he carefully says, letting me know it's cool if I don't want them tagging along.

"I promise. This," I say, waving my hands to indicate everything happening at our table, "has been really nice. I would really like it if you guys came. Unless you already had plans of your own. Then I completely understand," I say. It just occurred to me that maybe they already have plans and we are holding them up.

"If you're sure then we'd love to go with you guys." As soon as the words leave his mouth, AJ lets out a 'whoop' in excitement. The whole table laughs at how animated he is.

After we finish eating, Diesel pays the tab while I try to gather up all of my children's things. I try to get him to tell me how much it was so I can give him some money but he refuses. As we make our way outside, I thank him for paying.

I almost fall onto my ass when Diesel places Luke into his car seat, completely caught off guard by the move. As I put on my seatbelt after climbing in, I look back to make sure Sophia has hers on too before I start the engine. Once I see that Diesel and AJ are ready, I pull out of the parking lot towards the theatre. Tonight is turning out to be better than I thought it would be. Some great company truly makes a world of difference.

5

Diesel

While AJ and I follow behind Bella and her brood to the Holiday Drive-In, I think about everything that Bella told me tonight at the Pizza Palace. The woman has been put through the wringer by her selfish ex-fucking-husband. I don't think she truly realizes that. When she was telling me her story, she was trying to take on just as much of the blame as she was placing on him. I personally don't think the woman has anything to take the blame for. It seems like she made that man's life easier while he took full advantage of her sacrifices.

Fucker.

The more time I spend with Bella tonight, the more attractive I find her. She seems too good to be true. The woman has the body of a goddess but without all the superficial bullshit. Her kids are great too and are really working their way under my skin.

When she turns off the boulevard, I start to get concerned that something is wrong. This way doesn't lead to where we're supposed to be going. She finally pulls into a nice subdivision on the upper east side. She pulls into a driveway just as its garage door begins to lift and before I can shut off my bike, Sophia is hopping out of the backseat and racing into the house like her ass is on fire. Bella slides from the driver's seat and as she walks in our direction, I once again feel something inside my chest shift. She truly is a beautiful woman.

"Sorry, we had to stop real quick. Soph forgot to grab her dinosaur before we left the house earlier and we can't possibly see this movie without it," she says rolling her eyes, but the playful smile on her face tells the truth. She isn't upset at all that our plans are being slightly altered. Her calm demeanor is contagious and I find I don't mind the minor hiccup either when usually something like this would most likely annoy me.

"Dad," AJ whispers over my shoulder.

"Yeah?" I ask, turning my head so I can hear him better.

"I need to use the bathroom," he says, looking a little embarrassed.

"Can he use your bathroom, babe?" I ask, knowing AJ is too shy to ask for himself.

"Of course! Come on, AJ. I'll show you where it is," Bella tells my boy as she reaches her hand out to him as he climbs from behind me. I can't explain exactly what it is or how I know, but she is going to be something special to us. I don't know if it's in the gentle smile on her face that is only for him or her steering hand. It's definitely something in the way she ruffles his hair after removing his helmet for him. All of it does some strange shit to my heart. She is gentle with my boy, even after only just meeting him. The exact same way she is with her own kids, and it's my undoing.

I hop off my bike and go to stand next to her truck since Luke is still inside, while also watching her lead AJ into her house. There's no stopping the smile that takes over my face when Luke's eyes light up from seeing me. It only gets bigger when I hear Bella and AJ laugh as Sophia shrieks excitedly about something. A couple of minutes later, the three of them come back outside and we once again loaded up and are ready to go. Bella and her kids lead the way as I follow behind them through town.

Once we turn into the theater, I pull ahead and pay for all of our tickets. When we make our way around to the screen that will show our movie, I stop so Bella can back into a spot. As soon as she has maneuvered herself back into it, I park my bike next to her Tahoe and help AJ climb off. AJ and I store our helmets in my saddlebag as Bella starts hauling all kinds of shit out of the back end of her SUV.

I watch in amazement as she pulls out folding camping chairs, an air mattress, and a pump. This is followed by a large beach bag overflowing with snacks and a cooler with what I can only assume holds cold drinks. Then she walks around to the passenger side door and pulls out another massive bag with small pillows and blankets bursting from the top.

"What the fuck?" I mumble under my breath. Bella, the beauty, is without a doubt prepared. She's brought everything imaginable to ensure her children will enjoy the movie in comfort. This woman fascinates the shit out of me, and I'm desperate to know more about her.

"Whoa," AJ says. He's just as amazed at all the shit Bella

has pulled from the trunk of her SUV. It's like she's Mary-fucking-Poppins. Sophia doesn't seem phased in the slightest by her mother's endless preps. This is more than likely something they do often. I don't think I have ever seen someone this prepared for anything.

"I don't want to ever be a momma. It's wayyyy too much work," Sophia tells AJ, as she continues watching her mother in action.

"You're not kidding," he whispers back. I chuckle at the look of awe still on his face at all the shit she's brought along.

"You have a bug on your shirt, AJ, but it looks great," Sophia says without missing a beat. She turns her eyes to his after focusing on a spot on his shirt. I'm confused though because I don't see anything.

"What? Get it off!" he yells.

"I swear to all that is holy, Sophia Grace, if you lie to one more person about bugs being on them and make them freak the heck out, I'm going to ground you from your tablet for a year." With her hands on her hips and her eyes narrowed in warning, Bella scolds her mini clone.

"Sorry," Sophia tells AJ without a single ounce of remorse as she tries to use her cuteness to her advantage.

"Um, want me to blow up the air mattress, babe?" I ask, not sure what I need to do to help get things set up.

"That would be great. While you do that, I'll get Luke out of his car seat," she says as she's already opening his door and unbuckling him. Bella sets him in the cargo area of her truck to keep him out of everything while we finish setting up.

The realization hits me that Bella is such a natural at

doing all of this shit because she's always had to be. The man who should have been helping to make life easier fell down on the job and that pisses me off more than I care to admit. She's prepared for anything because nobody's ever had her back to help her juggle two children. I have a whole new appreciation for this woman that's been thrown curveball after curveball and still keeps swinging. I decide at that moment that even though I don't know Bella all that well yet; I want to be the person in her corner that she can call on. The person she goes to when she needs help. I don't know what it is about this woman, but something about her calls to me and I know deep down she's meant to be mine somehow.

It takes about fifteen minutes but I finally get the air mattress blown up and the kids have covered it in pillows and blankets. They are sprawled out like royalty watching the movie's trailer on Sophia's tablet. Bella and I kick back in the camping chairs as we watch our kids bond over dinosaurs.

Even with the age gap, they seem to get along as if they've never known a time without each other. It's like they've always been a part of each other's life. This is what I always imagined it would have been like if I'd found someone and had more children. As the thought crosses my mind, I look over at the beauty sitting next to me and can't help but think that just maybe my chance hasn't passed me by completely.

"Momma, can we have the bag with the chips and candy?" Sophia asks.

"Yeah. Do you guys want a drink too? We have Sprite, water, and juice pouches."

Both kids decide on juice and dive into the bag of goodies as soon as she sets it between them. In the blink of an eye, our kids are passing around a bag of Doritos and a Tupperware bowl of brownies. I watch them do this for long moments and it's like they've choreographed this through years of practice.

"Thanks for all of this, Bella. AJ doesn't get to do a lot of stuff like this when he's with his mother. I know it means a lot to him." She has no idea how her care and motherly vibe are impacting AJ. When King's sister does sweet things for him like this, he talks about it for weeks because it's such a foreign concept to him that women are usually caring and nurturing creatures. His experience with women is mostly from his mother and she isn't that way towards anyone but herself.

"It's truly my pleasure. Don't take this the wrong way, but this is what I always pictured my family would have been like. I thought it was supposed to be like this, but it just never happened with Trevor."

"I was just thinking the same thing while I was sitting here watching our kids. Everything just seems very natural with them. It's nice," I tell her because I understand exactly what she means. She gives me the sweetest smile at my agreement.

Once the sun has finally set, the screen flickers to life and we settle in for the double feature. It's a few minutes later when Luke decides he's had enough of playing with his toys and being cooped up in the back end of Bella's truck. At his squawk, I grab him under his arms and lift him out. When I try to set him on his feet, he squeezes me around my neck. It's the sweetest thing as he once again lets me know he doesn't want me to put him down.

Lifting him up, I hold him close to my chest and settle back into my chair. He fists my shirt as his body begins to relax, and in a matter of minutes, he's sound asleep and drooling on my shoulder. This little guy is probably the sweetest kid I've ever met. Having him cling to me makes me miss having kids underfoot that are this little. AJ was constantly in awe of everything he learned and experienced at this age and I wonder if Luke is the same.

Before I even realize what I'm doing, I pull Luke in tighter, place my palm around his little head, and place a kiss on his forehead. Shit, I shouldn't have done that. Glancing over, I catch Bella wiping a tear from her cheek.

"Sorry," I whisper, not wanting her to think I'm some kind of weirdo.

"It's fine," she whispers back and waves her hand, dismissing my worry.

"Thank you." As she nods to her son nestled against my chest, a sense of peace and rightness washes over me. I don't think anything could wipe the grin from my face.

Somehow. Someway. I'm going to make Bella and her brood mine.

6

♥ Bella ♥

I WATCH Diesel from the corner of my eye. The way he's holding my son protectively in his arms as he places a kiss on his head. I can't control the emotions that surge through me. My son is supposed to have this with his own father and here is a man we just met, giving it freely to Luke. Diesel has been this way with my son since the moment Luke mistakenly called him Daddy. And to Diesel's credit, he's just rolled with the punches.

He must always be in tune with what's going on around him because before I can blink, he's wrapping his free arm around my shoulders and offering me comfort. Somehow he must know this is what I need at the moment. Accepting the gesture, I lean my head on his shoulder and soak in the warmth that's radiating off of him. Turning my face farther into him, I close my eyes and breathe in traces of sandalwood and spice. The fragrance is intoxicating, and I just barely suppress the moan that's threatening to escape. Everything about him screams masculine and safe, and I can't stop wondering what it would be like for this man to be mine. It's been over a year since my divorce, and it's acceptable to want to move on to something new. It's been way too long since I've even entertained the idea of letting another man into my life. Diesel does seem to check a lot of my boxes.

What the hell am I even thinking about? He probably isn't interested in an overworked single mother. Don't get me wrong, I've had men show interest. But the second they learn I have two kids waiting on me at home, that quickly dies.

Pulling away from the sexy man, I get my thoughts trained back on my children and making sure they have everything I can possibly give them. When the kids scream at a dramatic part in the movie, I focus back on the screen and enjoy the evening for as long as it last.

"See you tomorrow, girl," I yell across the parking garage to Stacie. We just finished a long twelve-hour shift and I'm starving. It surprised me when Trevor actually showed up this morning to pick up the kids for his weekend visitation. I already had Paige on standby in case he pulled another no-show like he's been doing lately. He's so selfish and doesn't realize how much it hurts the kids when he bails on them at the last minute. All he's doing is teaching the kids that they can't depend on or trust the things he says.

I wave to Stacie when she drives by as I'm climbing into my Tahoe. My stomach lets out an embarrassingly loud growl as I click my seatbelt into place. As I start the engine I decide that I could really go for a chimichanga meal from Casa Rosa. Yeah, that's exactly what I need tonight especially since there's nobody to go home to tonight.

As I pull out of the parking garage I think about needing to hurry up and find a rental for us to move into. We close in two weeks and I'll only have twenty-four hours after I sign the papers to be out of the house. There just aren't enough hours in a day to get everything done. Especially when I've been having to do it all alone.

Once I pull into the restaurant's parking lot, I kill the engine and grab my wallet from my bag. I double check that I've locked the doors and as I turn to walk towards the entrance of Rosa's, a loud whistle pierces the air. The sound causes me to stop and turn around. To my surprise it's Diesel who's the culprit. Having caught my attention, he jogs towards me with that signature grin on his handsome face.

"Hey stranger," he says in that sexy southern drawl that has all sorts of naughty thoughts racing around my brain.

"Hey yourself. We've gotta stop meeting like this," I tell him and smile at how we seem to keep running into each other at restaurants. I glance behind him and don't see AJ, Looks like neither of us has our kids in tow tonight.

"Not on your life, babe. Care to have dinner with me?" he asks. I'll be damned. If I'm not mistaken, the man is flirting with me. Game on buddy because I really want to know more about you.

"I can't think of anything else I'd rather do," I say. But that's a total lie. I can think of about a half dozen things I'd like to do with this man, and trust me, not one of them includes a restaurant filled to the brim with people. All my thoughts involve being naked in the privacy of a bedroom. The thought instantly causes my cheeks to heat, but in my defense, it's been a really long time since I've been with a man.

"Oh beauty, I like the way you think," he says while smirking at the blush that has overtaken my cheeks. Only making them heat more. I've always worn my thoughts and emotions on my face so he probably realizes that something inappropriate has crossed my mind.

"Where's AJ tonight?" I ask as he's opening the door and gestures for me to go ahead of him. A gentleman. I like it. Before he can answer, though, Rosa is rushing towards us and her whole face lights up when she notices that we've come in together.

"Bella! Diesel! Si`, he is a good man. He will take care of you," she tells me. Her Spanish accent is thick with emotion as she grabs my hands and pulls me in for one of her motherly hugs. What can I say? I'm a regular around here and it seems Diesel is as well.

"I'd never make her cry," Diesel tells her, but his eyes never leave mine. I feel like he's making a promise. Maybe even a statement and I'm not entirely sure what to make of this man he's showing me tonight. He's a lot flirtier and seems more forward tonight. Without our kids around as a buffer, the undeniable sexual tension is palpable.

Rosa motions for us to follow her and leads us over to a large corner booth. She relays the specials for the night as she places the menus on the table and then rushes off to grab our drinks. It's nice coming here because she always knows what I want. On the nights that I come in alone, I can sit down and she takes care of everything. It seems she must know Diesel's usual as well since she didn't ask him what he wanted. Something about knowing that he frequents this local hidden gem has me appreciating him even more.

As I slide into the booth, I'm a little surprised when Diesel slides in next to me instead of taking the bench across from me. When our thighs touch under the table, as innocent as the contact is, I admittedly get a little flustered. I seriously need to get laid. The man is making me a horny wreck and he hasn't even touched me.

"To answer your earlier question, AJ is at his mom's house this weekend. I usually have him on Tuesday and Wednesday nights, and every other weekend. Where's your crew at tonight?" he asks, studying my face as he waits for me to reply.

"They're at their dad's house for the weekend." I leave out the part where it was a miracle he actually showed up. I don't want to speak badly about Trevor when he's finally doing what he's supposed to.

"So, do you come here a lot? I noticed Rosa knew you by name and didn't bother asking you what you wanted to drink, either," he laughs having also caught that little tidbit.

"I come here at least once a week after a long shift at the hospital," I say as I reach for a chip.

"This is my go-to spot, too," he tells me, grabbing a chip for himself.

Rosa returns with our drinks and we both laugh as she sets down two tall MGD draft beers. "Your usuals?" She asks and we both nod as we take a long sip of the ice-cold brew.

"I'm guessing this is one of those nights that you just get off work?" he asks, tilting his head to the side and watching me closely.

"Yeah. You?" I ask as I grab a chip. I'm sure he can see just how exhausted I am.

"I did. I had an appointment that ran over tonight after a client changed his mind about what he wanted once he showed up. If it hadn't been for that I probably wouldn't have run into you tonight." For some reason, the thought of not seeing him tonight is disheartening. I don't think I'm ready to dissect exactly why that is. I'm already feeling overwhelmed by how drawn to him I seem to be and looking too closely at these feelings will only cause unnecessary stress in my already hectic life.

He starts quietly laughing and shaking his head. He's looking at me like he can't believe something and my curiosity finally wins out. I raise a brow in question, wanting to know what he finds so funny. "What?"

"Nothing. I'm sorry. I was just wondering if there's anything you don't make look good. You're in the standard hospital scrubs and you're still the prettiest woman I've ever seen." The honesty in his voice and the flirty grin on his face finally does me in.

"Thanks. I think?" I tell him, feeling my cheeks heat from the impact of his compliment and because of that grin. Good God, he doesn't play fair at all.

"Shit. I didn't mean to embarrass you. I'm sorry, it's just that there's something about you and I'm clearly out of practice when it comes to this kind of thing. Shit, I'm messing this all up."

"No! I'd say you're doing just fine," I tell him honestly and attempt a flirty grin of my own.

"I'm a little out of practice myself but what you're doing is working for me," I try to joke so that he doesn't feel alone with being out of his depth here.

Ten minutes later, Rosa is bringing out matching plates of food. Chimichangas with a side of rice and refried beans. I laugh at our identical "usual" as he knocks me off my axis when he leans over and whispers into my ear, "you're fucking perfect, baby," causing a shiver to race through my body.

Baby, that's new, he usually calls me babe. It's been a long time since anyone's called me baby and dang, it feels so good to hear it coming from this sexy as sin man's mouth.

Diesel should really come with a warning label. *Warning ovaries will explode when he flashes a flirty smile.* I'm pretty sure mine are preparing to carry his babies as we sit here eating dinner together. I was not prepared for a man like him, but I like how he makes me feel. It's been too long since I've felt appreciated. Like I'm worth the time and effort. I don't think he realizes the more he reminds me of what it feels like to be a woman again, the more I want him. He's giving me pieces of myself back that I hadn't even realized were missing. The last year and a half has been hard, but I'm more than just a mom and nurse; I'm a desirable woman.

"Back 'atcha, handsome," I tell him, deciding to go for it and to stop playing it safe. Biting my lip, I look up from my plate to find him looking down at me with obvious interest and no small amount of heat behind his eyes. Clearing his throat, he refocuses on his plate saying, "let's dig in before it gets cold."

We sit in comfortable silence as we eat our meal, sharing brief glances and only stopping briefly for sips of our cold beer. It's really nice and before I know it, we've spent three hours talking about anything and everything. I feel honored to know all about Alex "Diesel" Logan. He got his nickname from the guys he worked with years ago because of his strength and size. He tells me all about his life. From how he met AJ's mother, their time together, and how and why they ended. I learn about what led him to where he is today. He shares how he bought and renovated his home. He is an open book, and it's refreshing to have a man share his thoughts and feelings with me. Instead of sneaking around and hiding things from me like Trevor always did.

He asks about how I met Trevor, so I tell him. I confess how we married young, the struggles of being pregnant, and then juggling being a new mom while trying to finish college. I confide in him that I had no idea my husband was unhappy because I was too exhausted to notice. Diesel doesn't judge me for any of it. He even made me feel better when he told me it was Trevor that had an obligation to tell me when he felt like things were slipping in our marriage. How he should have been upfront with me so that we could have worked together to fix what was broken. In fact, he was adamant that Trevor should have brought his worries to the table to work through instead of someone else's bed. He's right, I'm not a mind reader and there was no way for me to know what he was feeling without him first sharing.

His words showed me he is a good man, one who wouldn't cheat even if given the opportunity. He's the kind of man that would work hard to make things right if they started to crumble. He asks me about working in the ER and the people I work with. We share stories of our youth and the stupid stuff we did as kids who didn't know any better. I tell him about losing my parents when I was eighteen and how the only person I have left in my family is my cousin Paige. We talk about how awesome we think our kids are and that we both noticed that they seemed to jump right in as if they'd always know each other.

The whole time we're talking, we migrate closer and closer toward each other. When we're as close as we can get, Diesel wraps his arm around my shoulder and pulls me into his side as we continue to chat. Every time we discover something else we have in common; he drops a soft kiss atop my head and admittedly I find the move perfect. With each kiss and gentle squeeze from him, it starts to feel more and more natural. This thing that's happening between us feels good and familiar. It's like we've known each other for ages and not the short time it's actually been.

When Rosa comes by with our checks, we realize how long we've been holed up in our booth. It was so easy to get completely lost in each other. I really like this man and hate that the evening is ending.

Diesel grabs both of our checks and hands Rosa a hundred-dollar bill for our meal. He tells her to keep the change and apologizes for us holding up the table for the last three hours. In our defense, the crowd died down hours ago, and we weren't preventing anyone from getting a table of their own.

"You two make such a cute couple. You make Rosa so happy that you're together. You come back and I make something special for you next time," Rosa tells us and neither of us corrects her for assuming that we're together romantically. We both are grinning when she walks back towards the front counter to cash out her other customers.

"I don't want this night to end," Diesel says as he gazes into my eyes. I've been thinking the same thing for the last hour and it's nice to know that I'm not alone. That neither of us knows how to proceed from here.

"I don't either," I tell him softly, not wanting to shatter the moment.

"I want you Bella, so bad. But not like this. I feel something happening between us. Something that could be the real deal and I don't want just some hookup with you. I want to do this the right way. Take you out on a date and really get to know each other. I want you to really trust me and know without a doubt I'm in this for all the right reasons." I feel a wave of hope from his confession. The fact his feelings mirror my own is everything I could hope for. He's right and I respect him for being honest because it would be a tragedy to ruin this thing and end up with regrets.

"Thank you," I whisper, "thank you for being such a good man, Diesel."

"Baby, if you knew what I wanted to do to you, I'm not so sure you'd think I was a good man. I know you're going to be worth the wait but let's get out of here before I change my mind. This is killing me but you're worth waiting for Bella. I hope you know how much I mean that."

Swooning, I'm truly swooning right now. Oh my god!

This man. Where the hell did he come from? I don't have a single doubt that every word he says is true. This thing between us feels like it could be something amazing if given proper care and attention. I'm struggling to hold back the tears that are threatening to spill from the overwhelming feelings.

"Ok." What more can I say? He's right. I don't want to ruin any chance at something great developing.

Sliding from the booth, he turns around and offers me his hand to help me up. I gasp when our fingers touch. I get a zap from the electricity that's surging between us. Darting my eyes to his, I can see that he feels it, too.

"Fuck," he growls low under his breath, causing a new surge of tingles to race up my spine. Shaking his head in disbelief with a crooked smile on his face, he links our fingers together and leads me outside.

When we reach my truck, I hit the button on my key fob and my doors unlock. When the lights inside flicker on it gives us a bit of light to see each other. Diesel maneuvers me so that my back's against the driver's door as he moves in closer. Bracing his arms above my head on the doorframe, he cages me in. He leans into me and presses his lips against my ear as he softly he says, "I want to see you again. You good with that?"

"More than good with that," I say, shuddering as he rubs his bearded chin against my cheek.

"Where's your phone, Bella? Need your number so we can figure out when we can get together next." He presses the sweetest kiss to my cheek before pulling back and wrapping his arms around my waist. Chest to chest, I can feel his hard length pressed against my belly. Holy shit, he's huge.

I'm frozen on the spot making him chuckle when he realizes I'm unable to form a coherent thought. I gotta give him credit, the man is smooth.

"Wait, what were we talking about?"

"Phone, baby," he repeats, smirking at me and effectively pulling me out of the Diesel-induced brain fog he created. Reaching into my pocket, I pull out my cell and type in his number as he rattles it off. Just to make sure he gets my number, I send him a text. Hearing the tone come from his back pocket, I know he got it.

"Send me a text when you get home so I know you made it there safely. Okay?"

"Okay," I say, getting sucked into his vortex once again as he leans in and places the softest kiss on my lips. I squeak when he squeezes my ass as he pulls me away from the door. Reaching around me, he pulls on the handle and opens the door as he pats my bottom. Taking the hint, I turn around and get inside.

"Diesel," I breathe as he slides his hand up my sides to my face. His thumb gently strokes across my cheek as he leans into my truck and presses his lips against mine once more. When his tongue flicks across the seam of my lips asking for entry, I open for him without hesitation. He takes control of the kiss as he tilts my face, pushing his tongue into my mouth and devouring me completely. There's no other way to describe it. I have no idea how much time passes before he finally drags himself away. From the look on his face, he's feeling the heat just as much as I am. We just lit the match, and I can't wait to feel the flames.

Pecking my lips a few more times, he backs away, then orders me to drive safely and not to forget to let him know I made it home in one piece. Nodding my head, I tell him that I'll text him as soon as I'm home. I watch as he reluctantly closes my door and moves towards his bike on the other side of the parking lot. I feel like a stalker as I at him while he puts his helmet on and starts the beautiful machine. I come out of my hypnotized state when I finally realize he's sitting there waiting for me to pull out.

7

Diesel

Climbing into bed, I look at the message I got a few minutes ago from Bella. As she promised, she let me know she has made it home safely. The first thing I do is save her number under *Beauty*. It's what I think of her every single time she crosses my mind. It's become abundantly clear that I really want her. I don't know how, but I will make her mine. After everything that we shared with each other tonight and that fucking kiss that about had me shooting off in my jeans like a kid seeing his first set of real tits; I have to have her. This woman will be my undoing. The promise of her has me excited and I can't wait to see what the reality will actually be like.

Beauty: Made it home safely. Climbing into bed to crash for the night. Hope you made it home okay. Night handsome.

Diesel: Lying in bed thinking about you, baby. Night. Sleep good.

Over the last week, I have thought about Bella and her brood a lot. We had such a good time at dinner and then at the movies. I can't remember ever having such a nice time hanging out with a woman and her kids. Actually, I think that's the only time I've hung out with a woman and a bunch of kids.

I also can't remember a time that I've felt this attracted to a woman. Even Charity, AJ's mom, didn't make me feel this way. She was a beautiful woman, sure, but she didn't have the sweetness and grace that Bella has. Not even close. Bella is in a league all of her own. She's beautiful with her long, lean body and all those curves in just the right places. She has a set of tits that can bring a grown man to his knees. High and round; you'd never imagine that she's had two kids. Don't even get me started on that tight ass that makes me want to grab a handful and hold on tight while I fuck her from behind. If I had to make a guess, Bella has a little Puerto Rican blood running through her veins. She has that tan complexion and a head full of dark brown hair with a few highlights from time in the sun. Her bright blue eyes pop against her sun-kissed skin. Her lips are pink and full and every time I look at them, I imagine what they would feel like wrapped around my dick. When I kissed her, she made these little moans that had me as hard as granite. I bet she's a wildcat in bed when she's lost in the moment. Yep, I am definitely feeling a strong attraction to this woman, but for once it's not just her looks drawing me in. Bella is the whole package. Sweet, loving, smart as hell, has her life together and is drop-dead gorgeous.

Her ex-husband was a fucking idiot to let a woman as sweet and beautiful as her slip through his fingers. There is no way he appreciated what he had if he could throw it all away so easily. I've only tasted her lips and I already know I could never let her go.

There's no question the woman is a knockout, but she's so much more than that. She was tender with her babies but firm when warranted. She's truly an amazing mother and anyone can see it just from spending a few moments in their presence.

I chuckle, thinking about the spitfire, Sophia. That little girl is something else. She will probably grow up to be beautiful just like her momma since she's already the spitting image. I can see her being the class clown. The kid can sling insults and random bullshit like nothing I've ever seen before. She could probably bullshit her way out of anything and leave you scratching your head wondering what in the fuck just happened. She's sassy, that's for sure, but I also watched the gentle way she had with her little brother. It didn't escape me that at only five years old, she was keeping an eye on her mother too. It doesn't surprise me one bit that she notices all the changes happening in their lives. Kids are smarter than anyone ever gives them credit for. They know when shit isn't right in their world.

Little Luke is something special too. The boy has a tender heart. If that isn't guarded and protected the damage could be detrimental. His father should have his ass beat for not being more involved with him. The little guy needs a man in his life to learn from. Someone to teach him how to a be good man when he grows up. It's a father's responsibility to teach his daughters what they deserve from all the men who will come into their lives in the future. To show their sons how to treat and respect women. Yeah, Trevor needs his ass beat for letting his children down.

I wasn't the only one whose heart was touched by the trio either. AJ has been talking about them nonstop since last Friday night. He'll randomly think about something that one of them said or did and start laughing about it. They impacted my boy in a good way. All three of our children have been let down by a parent. Only for AJ, it's his mother. Bella acted like more of a mother and was more nurturing in one evening than Charity has been his whole life. His mom is a selfish bitch who doesn't think about anyone but herself though, so comparing the two is impossible. There's no contest there. Bella would win hands down every single time.

Now that I think about it, AJ may have even been a little envious that Sophia and Luke have such an attentive mother like Bella. If things go how I hope they will, he'll get more of that in his life soon enough. He could definitely benefit from having a strong woman like Bella in his life.

Bella works in the busy ER at Mercy General while raising two kids all by herself. That takes a lot of strength and fortitude. Strength, brains, and beauty. I would be lucky to have a woman like her as my own.

Thinking about all things Bella gets me hard. Taking my cock in my hand, I stroke one out to thoughts of her smile, tits, ass, and those luscious lips I hope to make mine soon. Within minutes I find my release and come all over my stomach with her name falling from my lips like a prayer. I lay there for a moment to catch my breath before getting up and heading for the shower. After I get myself clean, I throw on a pair of athletic shorts and go to the kitchen to grab myself a beer from the fridge. When I walk into the room I find my dad perched on a bar stool, snacking on some leftover pizza, and drinking my cold beer.

"Old man, don't you have shit to eat and your own beer to drink next door in your own house?"

"I do, but yours is always better," he says barely lifting his face from his plate. Opening the fridge I grab the last cold MGD and make a mental note that I need to restock it as I twist off the cap and take a deep pull.

"Where were you at tonight? Thought you would have been home a couple of hours ago," he asks once he's finished stuffing his face.

"I went to dinner at Rosa's and ran into someone I knew. We sat around shooting the shit for a bit and then I came home. Why did you need something?" I ask him wondering why he's keeping tabs on me.

"No, just came by earlier to borrow your socket wrenches and you weren't here is all."

"Did you bring them back?" I ask him with a raised brow because he has a bad habit of taking off with my shit and not bringing it back. He doesn't do it intentionally; the man just has a severe case of ADHD and gets easily sidetracked.

"Yeah, put them back in the garage where I found them," he says which honestly shocks me that he brought them back.

"Weren't you supposed to have some woman come over and shack up for the weekend?" I know that's what he told me earlier today.

My dad is still young himself. At 48 years old and the man loves women. He and my mom got pregnant with me when they were in high school. I don't remember much but

I do know they had tried to make things work. They hadn't been dating when he knocked my mom up. They just hooked up from time to time and I was a product of them being young and dumb. My mom took off when I was about six, and my dad did what he had to do and raised me by himself when he was still just a kid himself.

For as long as I can remember, the man has never lacked female attention or company and it's surprising that I don't have a bunch of brothers and sisters running around this town somewhere. I'm always telling him it's not too late to start over and find himself a good woman to settle down with. I think somewhere in the back of his mind he wants that, but he doesn't want to ever go through what he went through with my mom again. When she left it gave him some major trust issues. He spends time with them and shacks up with them for a weekend here and there, but what he won't do is let them stick around. Once he's had his fill, he sends them packing. It sounds bad, but in his defense, I think when he starts getting attached, he gets freaked out and bails before they can. Doesn't make it right, but I get why he does it.

"Nah, I told her not to come. I've been thinking about what you're always saying. About me settling down, and I'm giving the idea some serious thought. I'm getting too old to keep doing what I'm doing. Plus, it'd probably be okay to come home to the same woman every night. Let her cook me some good food and fuck me to sleep. King seems to enjoy having a steady woman around when he has one," he says, making me laugh at his interpretation of what a relationship looks like.

"I'm not so sure that what King does with the

"women" he keeps around is what you're looking for. And if it is, I don't want to know a damn thing about it," I say, emphasizing women with finger quotes. And if my dad is into the kink that King is into, I mean it when I say that I don't want to know anything about it.

King is one of the best dudes I know. He, his sister, and Crow grew up in foster care together. Whatever happened to him when they were growing up has made him the man he is today. He doesn't do so well if he isn't in complete control of everything going on in his life. The women King gets involved with are all submissive and while he doesn't talk about his relationships, I know he moves the women he sees into his house where they engage in a domestic discipline type of relationship. I've caught enough over the years to figure that much out. Yeah, if my dad is into that shit, I don't want to know.

"I'm not into the kinky shit that crazy bastard is," he says and laughs when he catches the look on my face. He knows I'm referring to King's control issues.

King has two other shops that are both a half hour's drive from the one we work out of and he micro-manages the shit out of them. His attention to them has made them very profitable, but I can imagine that if you're the person managing one of them, it makes it a little hard to do. I bet the Miami crew are glad he lives hours away so they don't have to deal with his hovering.

"I don't need to know what you do behind closed doors, old man. If you're serious about finding a good woman, I think you should go for it. I've been thinking the same things for myself lately," I confess.

"On that note, I'm going home. I don't want to know

what you do behind closed doors, either." He leaves all of his shit out on my bar and heads out the side door to go home. I chuckle at his quick retreat.

After cleaning up his mess, I go back to my room and fall back into bed. I have the best night's sleep I've had in ages, dreaming of a life with the beautiful Bella and our brood that we share.

8

♥ Bella ♥

I HAD such a great time with Diesel last night at Rosa's. I came home, fell right into bed, and dreamt about the tall, dark, and handsome man that has suddenly appeared in my life. I start to wonder when I'll hear from him. Will he make me wait? Is he really going to call or was he just trying to be nice? As I start to have doubts and begin to feel down that maybe I misread the situation, my phone pings.

Diesel: Mornin' baby

Bella: Good morning handsome

Diesel: Sleep good beautiful?

Bella: I did Dreamt about a tattooed hottie

Diesel: Trying to make me jealous?

Bella: LOL Never You were the star in my dreams

Diesel: Do tell

Bella: No time mister I have to get up and get ready for work

Diesel: Bummer ☹ all right have a good shift let me know when your next day off is

Bella: I will TTYL xoxo

Floating on air, I make my way to the bathroom to get ready for my shift.

I won't say or think it because then we'll get swamped. However, with the current lull in patients, I'm able to sit down at the nurses' station and get a jump start on patient charts. My hope is that I can get out of here on time tonight when my shift actually ends. Which will only be eight more hours if I can stay caught up on paperwork. That's a big if, though. It's more likely than not that we'll get slammed and that will go all to hell. There is no such thing as getting ahead when you work in the emergency room of a busy hospital like Mercy General.

I smile thinking about the texts that Diesel sent to me this morning. I feel like a teen with her first crush. He's turning out to be a better man than I could have ever imagined. He's kind and sweet and there's no denying that the man is sexy as sin. Tall and broad, with all those tattoos. He makes my heart flutter every time I think about how it might be to have a man like him as my own. I hope he's really as interested as he seems to be because I don't think I could handle another man giving me false hope after what Trevor put me through.

"What has you smiling, Ms. Bella?" My good friend and co-worker Stacie is smiling down at me with a knowing look on her face.

"I met a man," I say with wide eyes.

"What!? You didn't tell me you were seeing anyone. That's great news, Bella," She says excitedly.

"It's really new and technically we haven't even gone out on a first date yet. We met when I helped Paige move into her new apartment and then ran into each other again at the Pizza Palace. We both were with our kid and he and his son ended up sitting with us because the place was a madhouse and there weren't any other tables available. We had such a good time that they wound up going with us to the drive-in that night too. Then last night after I left here I stopped in at Rosa's and he was walking in at the same time I was. We ended up having dinner together and spent three hours just talking and getting to know each other. I really like him, Stacie. And that is scaring the crap out of me. We exchanged numbers before going our separate ways and he's sent a few text messages. But that's really all that's happened so far," I say, giving her the shortened version of how I met Diesel and AJ.

"Well, I hope it works out. You seem happier and lighter. I haven't seen you like this since long before you and Trevor divorced. You deserve to find a good man who will treat you like a queen. I always thought you were too good for Trevor. He never really appreciated you," she says gently. She knows Trevor has been a touchy subject for me. Stacie has stood by me through my entire divorce. She knows everything that I went through, and the impact it had on not only me but my kids as well. She's right though, I deserve to find someone who will make me and my children happy. I think meeting Diesel has helped solidify that I'm finally over my ex. And that feels like progress.

"Incoming ladies. We've got a couple of buses en route from the pileup on the highway," our CNO (Chief Nursing Officer) tells us before shouting, "I need all my available trauma nurses ready to go in the next couple of minutes. Let's make a difference, people."

While I hate that anyone ever needs to come in like this; I live for the thrill I get when it's go-time. The fast pace of the Emergency Room is what drew me to specialize in trauma and critical care. We have a hospital full of amazing nurses and we are without a doubt a special breed, but not everyone is cut out to handle the stress and pressure that comes with making life-altering decisions on the fly. I have always been able to compartmentalize my emotions and everything becomes hyper-focused during those intense moments when someone is rolled in and placed within our care.

The first paramedic brings in an adult female and a child, and the other bus brings in a single adult male. Upon arrival, everyone jumps into action to access patients and take vitals. Tests are ordered and wounds are treated. All the patients that were brought in have only minor cuts and bruises and can leave hours later when all their tests show nothing else is wrong.

With only half an hour left in my shift, I once again find myself at the nurses' station praying that we don't get hit again before I get to leave. For the rest of my shift, I spend time getting everyone's charts updated and making sure everything is ready for shift change. When my replacement shows up, I update her on the patients currently under our care. Ten minutes after that, I'm grabbing my purse from my locker and headed towards the parking garage.

"See ya tomorrow morning, girlie," Stacie shouts as she approaches her car. This is our routine when we get off work.

"See ya in the morning, Stace," I call back, opening my door and climbing inside so that I can make the trek home. Sadly, to an empty house.

Once I got home, I make a frozen dinner in the microwave and work on cleaning up the house. My goal is to get the laundry caught up before the kids come home tomorrow night. Once I'm finished with all of my chores, I make my way into the bathroom and submerge myself in a hot bath with a glass of wine. The hot water feels like heaven as it works to soothe my tired body.

Looking at my phone that's sitting on the edge of the tub, I debate on calling Diesel. He said he usually works long hours during the weekends when he doesn't have AJ. I don't want to bother him in case he's busy with a client. But... I could send a quick text and then he could look at it when he had the time and would know I had been thinking about him. Plus, he asked for me to let him know when I had my next day off.

I chew on my thumbnail as I contemplate what I should even say if I do text him. Maybe I should just wait until tomorrow. I am so bad at this shit. As an adult, I have never had to do the whole dating thing. I was young when Trevor and I got together and I've forgotten how to go about getting to know someone new. I don't know what the protocol for a new relationship is but after another few minutes of driving myself crazy, I decide to just go for it.

Bella: Hey Handsome. Home from work and enjoying a hot bath after a crazy day. My next day off is Monday

Diesel: Been thinking about you all fuckin' day baby. I'm off on Wednesday. I'll have AJ. I don't mind doing something with our kids. Up to you.

Diesel: Gotta run. next client is coming in now. Sweet dreams beauty. Catch up with you in the morning.
Bella: Night Handsome. XOXO

Closing out my text messages, I scroll through my contacts and hit call when I reach the number I'm looking for. It only rings once before her greeting has me groaning.

"What up, biotch!?"

"Seriously Paige? You're a grown ass woman who is going to be a flipping lawyer and you answer the phone like you're thirteen," I tell her, trying to hold back my giggle.

"Hells-bells, haven't you learned by now that I don't give two shits what anyone thinks about me? Nobody ever gave us anything and we don't have to try and live up to what anyone else thinks. There's not a single reason that we should feel like we have to curb who we are. Or be some sort of false impression of who we really are. We don't answer to anyone so stop worrying about what people think and start taking the world by the balls. Lord knows that's what I'm doing."

"Geez, okay. That got deep really fast. You ok sweetie?" I ask her.

"I'm fine," she sighs, making me think maybe she isn't all that fine. "I'm just lonely. Between school, studying, and work there isn't much time for going out and meeting a man. If something doesn't change soon I am going to have to swipe left to find a hookup. What's new with you? How's the house hunting coming along?"

She quickly changes the subject completely, so I can't dive deeper into what is going on with her. Taking it for the hint that it is, I leave the topic of her being lonely alone for the time being.

"Oh god, Paige. There is absolutely nothing available out here in Gulfport that isn't something that should have been condemned years ago. You lucked out finding the apartment you're in. I really don't want to but I may have to look in Biloxi. That puts me farther away from my work and the kid's schools though. I could see what's available in Lyman. Lyman isn't necessarily bad, but it would also put me farther out than I am now. If I was able to buy something, that would be a whole different story. That's out of the question though since Trevor the jackass destroyed our credit. That option is completely off the table for at least another year." The market is really crappy right now and I may have to move farther out than I want to be, but it's starting to look like I won't have a choice if my realtor can't find me something soon.

"You guys are more than welcome to come and stay with me if you need to. It would be a little cramped, but we could make it work," she offers. I know she's right and we could make it work, but it would be extremely cramped with four people living in her two-bedroom apartment. Not to mention she just established her independence and I don't want to do anything to infringe upon that. It's important for her to have her own space without us in her way. I'm just going to have to look into the neighboring towns to see what will work for us that is in my price range. It will all work itself out. I hope.

"I appreciate the offer and if I can't come up with any other options, you may have some unwanted houseguests. I still have a week to find something, so hold that thought for now."

"You got it, Hells-bells. Listen, I have to jet. I'm on in

ten minutes. Call me tomorrow night and we'll figure out a time to get together and have dinner."

"Will do. Love you, Paigie-Poo."

"Love you to infinity and beyond, Hells-bells."

We both laugh as we end our call. I'm so proud of her. She's been working her ass off for the last four years. She works on the weekends as an exotic dancer, so she can pay her way through law school. I know some people may look down on her for the job choice, but it allows her to work around her school schedule. She's been only working on the weekends and it doesn't hurt that she can put a lot of cash into savings. She hasn't had to take out a single student loan to help cover any of her school costs. I'd say being able to graduate debt free is worth the comments she may get from small-minded jerks from time to time.

My pruned hands and the tepid water let me know it's time to get out and dry off so that I can get ready for bed. I have one more twelve-hour shift in the morning to make it through, but then I'm off for the next four days.

As I'm drying off, I wonder if Diesel and AJ would be interested in having dinner Wednesday night with me and the kids. I'll have to ask him about it tomorrow when we have more time to talk. With the kids being gone to their dad's house, I don't bother putting my pajamas on and settle for climbing into my bedroom naked. As I lay here, I replay my dream from last night in my head. My heart rate picks up as I slide my hands across my belly and my pussy clenches when I move my hand up to cup my breast as I slide the other down. My center is drenched, hot and slick from sliding my finger between my folds. I pinch my nipple and roll my thumb across my clit as I picture Diesel's hands on my body. A moan escapes my lips when I slide my fingers inside. My back bows and my breathing becomes labored as I imagine his hands and mouth on me. I pant and whimper as my body heats, racing closer to finding bliss. I almost find it when my phone starts to ring. I groan in frustration, feeling like I could cry because I was so close.

When I grab my phone from the nightstand, I see Diesel's name across the screen and quickly answer.

"Hello?" I cringe when my breath is still labored from my almost orgasm.

"Baby? Why are you out of breath? Everything ok?" he asks, his voice laced with concern.

"Umm....?" My cheeks heat from embarrassment because I can't tell him I was getting myself off to thoughts of him. He's quiet for a long moment before realization must hit him.

"Babe. Were you being a bad girl?" he chuckles but his voice is smug

"Don't tease me. I can't help it. You got me all worked up, and it's been a really long time since a man has even kissed me," I whine as I start to feel self-conscious about admitting that.

"I'm sorry. Were you already in bed?"

"Yeah."

"What are you wearing, baby?" His voice is deeper and I can tell he's turned on, probably because he caught me in the act.

"Nothing," I whisper and start panting again. This game has me getting just as excited as he seems to be.

"Put your phone on speaker and tell me what you were doing before I interrupted you," he growls. Doing as he asks, I put my phone on speaker and place it on the pillow next to me.

"I climbed into bed and was thinking about how it would feel to have your hands on me. I cupped my breast and slide my finger into my pussy and I was rubbing my clit," I pant and moan, doing everything I'm describing.

"Fuck baby. Pinch your nipple hard. Tug on it like it's my hands working your body. Slide your finger into that tight, wet pussy. Let me hear how my hands feel working your body," he says as he too is breathing harder.

I do as he says, groaning in pleasure as I get closer to finding my release. I can hear his bike in the background but pay it no attention. He must be using the Bluetooth in his helmet; the hum of his bike is getting me hotter.

"Oh god, Diesel. I'm so close," I cry, breathing hard as I thumb my clit harder and push my fingers in and out of my core faster and harder.

"Diesel!" I wail, calling out his name as I hurdle over the edge. I lay here sweaty and out of breath as I slowly come down from my orgasmic high. The roar of his bike disappears into silence and a moment later there's a knock at my door.

"Open the door, baby. I'm outside," he tells me before hanging up. It takes me a second to understand what he just said, but when it clicks that he's at my door, I quickly hop up and throw on my pink silk robe. I race down the hall to the front door and swing it open. Standing there is my every fantasy come to life. His eyes are hooded, his nose flared, and his chest rises quickly like he could breathe fire. Stepping inside, he throws the door closed and lifts me into his arms as he slams his lips on mine. I wrap my arms and legs around him quickly as our mouths fuse together in a long, deep kiss that seems to go on forever. He grinds his hard length into my swollen nub when my back hits the wall. Lifting me higher, he uses his big body to hold me in place as he works his cock free from his jeans and lines himself up. Wasting no time, he thrusts into me and sets a steady pace as he moves inside me. Burying his face in my neck, he pounds into my body faster.

"Fuck baby. You feel so goddamn good," he groans.

I roll my hips, searching for friction and causing my clit to rub against him as he propels us toward the finish line. Holding onto my waist, he tilts his hips and pulls me down into his upward thrusts. The strength this man possesses is unimaginable.

"Diesel! Oh God, honey! I'm so close, don't stop," I beg.

"Whose pussy is this, Bella?" he growls.

"Yours. It's yours," I moan. I'd tell him anything he wants as long as he doesn't stop what he's doing.

"That's right. This pussy is fucking mine," He says through clenched teeth as we both come long and hard together.

I tighten my arms around him and breathe heavily into his neck. Desperately trying to catch my breath. When my back hits something soft, I lift my head and see that he's carried us into my bedroom. I'm so blissed out that I never even noticed we were moving. I whimper when he pulls out, not wanting to lose the connection. His eyes dart to mine then back to my core where he watches, mesmerized, as his come leaks from inside me. The look of awe stretched across his handsome face, quickly morphs into one of panic.

"Shit babe, I forgot a condom," he says worriedly.

"I'm on the pill and I'm clean. I got tested two years ago after I found out Trevor had been cheating. Since then, I haven't been with anyone," I tell him honestly.

"I'm clean too. Has a physical a month ago for my life insurance. I was tested then and I haven't been with anyone since either," he says as he removes his clothes and climbs back between my thighs. I'm amazed how his cock is still just as hard as when he got here. He unties my robe and opens it as he rises onto his knees and looks over every inch of my body.

"You're so beautiful," he whispers reverently, as he runs his rough hands across my skin. Diesel trails his finger from the hollow of my neck, down my sternum, between my breasts, and down. He cups my pussy before lazily circling my clit with his thumb. I'm shocked when he palms my pussy possessively, causing my breath to hitch as he wakes my body up again.

"This is mine, baby, isn't it? You gave it to me, and it's mine now," he says, never taking his eyes off his hand as his finger moves faster. I need more contact, more friction but the hold he has on me prevents me from moving.

"Yes," I moan in frustration. I need to move. I grip the sheets in my hands and throw my head back, writhing as I come again.

He flips me onto my belly and slams into me as I pulse around his thrusting cock. He pulls my hips up and pulls me into his forward thrusts. Moving one hand to the back of my neck, he presses my cheek to the bed as he squeezes my hip tightly, no doubt leaving a mark behind. With a final thrust, he presses his hips into me as he roars his release. The intensity sending me soaring once again. I come all over him as his cock pulses and he fills me. Rocking his hips, he gently glides in and out, milking every ounce of pleasure from me.

"It's so hot watching my cum slide out of your pussy," he says as he uses his finger to try and push his seed back inside me. Watching my face, he rims my puckered hole with his wet finger and the move causes me to tense. I've never had anyone touch me there, so I wasn't expecting him to do it.

"Gonna fuck you here soon." Slipping the tip of his finger inside my bottom, unexpectedly a moan slips from my lips. I'm surprised when the idea doesn't make me want to protest.

"You like that, babe, don't you?" Withdrawing his finger, he places a kiss on the small of my back as he climbs into bed next to me and pulls me against his sweaty body.

"We need a shower, Diesel," I whisper into his chest.

Nodding of his head, he climbs out of bed and hoists me into his arms as he takes us into the bathroom. A quick shower later and we both fall back into my bed where we pass out within minutes tangled in each other's arms.

9

Diesel

For the last ten minutes, we've been sitting around the reception area shooting the shit and waiting for our next clients to show up. My dad has been staring at me the entire time, not hiding his impatience mind you, when he finally grows a pair and asks what he's apparently been dying to know.

"So, AJ said you guys went out with some woman and her kids last Friday night. What's that all about?" The nosey bastard leans in like a gossiping hen, making me smirk. He's not a patient man so I'm sure he's been dying to get the scoop even though he could have just asked me a few days ago when he first found out and I would have told him. It's not like it's a big secret and we literally just talked the other night about women so he had every opportunity to ask me then.

Taking pity on him and his nosiness, I explain that I met her when I was helping King's new tenant upstairs move a cabinet and how her son had instantly taken to me. I tell him about running into her again at the Pizza Palace and our kids convincing us to take them to the movies together and then running into her again at Casa Rosa.

I purposely leave out how I went over to her house last night. That detail is just for me. Waking up wrapped around Bella this morning was better than anything I could have dreamed up. I hated that we had to get up and were unable to spend more time together. Her ex was bringing her kids home early this morning. She's not ready to explain to the kids or to her ex that we have started seeing each other yet. I wasn't sure how I felt about that at first but after hearing her out, I get it. If something happened and things don't work out, I'd just be another man leaving. I can respect her wanting to give it a little time.

"You like her," he says accusingly. The way he's making it sound like it's a bad thing is making my hackles rise.

"I do. I like her. She's different. She's nice and she's sweet. She's a wonderful mother to her kids and was great with AJ, too. It doesn't hurt that she's smokin' hot either." It pisses me off that he's making me feel like I need to defend myself for being interested in a woman who's the total package.

"Tell me about the chick upstairs, King. I saw her a few days ago and she's hot and her body is fucking banging, Bro," Crow teases, trying to change the subject and get King to divulge some details about his new tenant. Crow is our resident peacekeeper.

"She's a stripper," King tells him with a shit-eating grin. Crow has a history of taking home strippers that don't seem to understand the concept of a one-night stand. They have a tendency to come knocking on his door on day two and things usually get a little crazy from there. A slow grin takes over Crow's face but King shoots him down before he can get too excited.

"Don't get any ideas, fucker. Not only is she my tenant, but the girl is a law student. She'll have you brought up on sexual harassment charges faster than you can say the words. She was quick to clarify when I rented the place to her that she 'isn't some bimbo who thinks it's'... How did she put it? Oh yeah, 'glamorous to take her clothes off and shake her tits and ass for a bunch of horny bastards. It's a way to make bank so she can pay her way through school without going broke in the process.' I have to admit, while the girl is fuckin' gorgeous for sure, she's smart and has a good head on her shoulders, or so it seems."

"Have to give her props for doing whatever it takes to get what she wants in life. It's more than I can say for a lot of people," I say, thinking that the Cruze women seem to have that in common. They're not letting life get in the way of getting shit done and making a good life for themselves. If Paige is anything like her cousin, she'll be just fine making her dream of being a lawyer a reality.

I get zoned in to listening to King and Crow talk about a trade show that will be coming to the convention center in the next few months. I laugh at them bickering back and forth about some artist that may or may not be coming when my phone starts to ring. Pulling it from my pocket, I look at the screen but don't recognize the number.

"Hello?"

"Good evening, I'm calling from Mercy General. I'm looking for an Alex Logan. May I ask whom I'm speaking with?" A woman asks.

"This is Alex Logan."

"Mr. Logan, I'm sorry to have to bother you but Alex Logan Jr. has been admitted tonight. He arrived with a broken collarbone and a possible concussion. Your son is fine and will make a full recovery. However, we've been unable to locate Mrs. Logan. She brought him in but seems to have left the premises. We attempted to contact her to let her know he's being discharged, but the number appears to be disconnected. Alex Jr. informed us it would be better to call you to come and get him instead." I replay what she's just said and try to focus on the fact he's okay. Everything she's just said has me pissed the fuck off and starting to see red. That fucking bitch dumped my son off in the ER while he was hurt and left him to fend for himself. She could have called me to come up there so he didn't have to go through all of that alone. I'll fucking throttle that bitch the next time I see her. I'd never hit a woman, but she really tries my fucking patience.

"I'm on my way now. Can you tell my boy I'll be there in fifteen minutes please?" I ask, hoping she'll let AJ know he won't be alone much longer.

"I will. I'll have his discharge papers ready by the time you get here, Mr. Logan. Drive safely."

"Thank you, ma'am. I'll be there shortly," I tell her and hang up. Looking over at my dad, I tell him what the lady from the hospital just told me. I make a quick call to my last client of the night and let him know I have to reschedule because my son was in an accident and is in the ER. Thankfully the reschedule worked better for Sam and this shit isn't costing me a loyal client. I promise to call and give them an update once I get AJ home and find out what happened. Taking a deep breath, I try to calm down and slow my racing heart. Once I have gained a semblance of control, I make my way across town to the hospital. Taking long strides through the double sliding doors of the ER, I eat up the distance between me and my kid. I go straight to patient check-in and the nurse does a double take as she takes in my size and immediately jumps into action.

"Can I help you, Sir?" she asks.

"He's here for the patient in curtain two," the nurse sitting next to her says as she motions for me to follow her. "Bella told me to be expecting you. She's in with your son now keeping him company." Her friendly smile has me instantly liking the woman. I follow her down a long hallway and through a set of locked doors that open up into the triage section of the Emergency Room. I hear Bella and my boy laughing as we approach the last curtain and the sound causes me to deflate. The relief that he's really okay is unexplainable. Thank God he wasn't alone.

"Bella, I brought Mr. Logan back for his son," the nice nurse I've been following says as she opens the curtain. My heart clenches when I find AJ leaning back in the hospital bed wearing a shoulder stabilizer while Bella sits next to him holding his hand. The visual makes my chest tighten at how right they look together. His own mother couldn't be bothered to stay by his side, but here is this amazing woman, sitting sentry at his bedside.

I don't miss how she is rubbing his hand soothingly like the loving mom he deserves to have in his life.

"Dad!" AJ calls out loudly.

"What happened, kid?" I cringe at my tone, but I've been a wreck since getting the call he was here and alone at that. "Sorry," I quickly apologize. I don't want him to think he's done anything wrong because he sure as shit hasn't.

"All right, boy. Start from the beginning. I want to know exactly what happened to land you in this place. And where the hell is your mother?"

Bella gets up attempting to leave us in privacy but I stop her before she can get away. I pull her into my side, dropping a quick kiss on the top of her head and I can't help but appreciate the feel of her body curved into mine.

"Stay, baby. Please," I tell her, needing her comfort for what I'm about to hear that's sure to piss me off.

"Okay. Whatever you need," she tells me with a sad smile. She's clearly just as upset that my son is injured and his mom bailed. I am so grateful that she was here for AJ when he needed someone the most. AJ watches us with a look of approval. I had no doubt he would accept Bella with open arms. She's the kind of woman people gravitate towards.

AJ finally tells me what happened and if it wasn't for Bella squeezing my waist, I would probably already be out the door hunting Matt down.

Charity didn't say anything to her current fuck buddy about bringing AJ's game system back like she'd promised me she would. So AJ took it upon himself to tell Matt he wanted his shit back. Some things were said, and Matt thought for some reason that he had the authority to discipline my son. When he went after AJ; AJ took off, running away from him. Matt was unable to catch AJ, but when he got close enough, he shoved him which caused AJ to fall. He fell down the front steps of their house which landed him here in the ER with a concussion and a broken collarbone.

"I don't want to go back there, Dad. He's always hanging around our house and mooching off mom. She never says a word to him when he's mean to me either."

"You'll be coming home with me, kid. I'll see what I can figure out about getting full custody this time. But it's going to be a fight with your mother, AJ. You need to get prepared for that. It's going to get ugly. Are you going to be okay with that because I don't want to do anything that will make life harder for you, buddy?" I usually try not to say anything bad about AJ's mom but this will not be an easy fight. Charity has always fought dirty and I have no doubt she'll use anything she can to win.

"If you'd like, I can ask Paige to come by and give you some advice. She's a law student, but her focus is family law. She could at the very least tell you what to focus on and who you should speak with," Bella offers, trying to help as much as she can.

"All right, baby. I'd really appreciate that. If you could set up a time at her earliest convenience, that would be so helpful," I tell her. I'm so grateful for her support and input.

"No problem. I'll call her when I leave. I've actually been off shift for the last two hours, but I didn't want to leave AJ here alone. Let me go over his discharge papers with you, then I'll go grab my stuff and make that call," she says, once again proving how perfect she is. She's been off for two hours and stayed with AJ so he wouldn't be alone. She's not even his mother but you'd never know with how she's caring for him.

Ten minutes later, I've been advised of AJ's restrictions as Bella goes over what to look for with his concussion to ensure he doesn't get worse. She assures me that he already seems much better than when she came in two hours ago, which admittedly is a huge relief.

Once AJ is released, we wait outside while she hurries to grab her stuff. Five minutes later, she's gliding through the front doors in our direction and I feel a sense of pride that this beautiful and caring woman is mine. That feeling of pride quickly turns to aggravation when every man she passes does a double take to get a look at her sexy self. It momentarily pisses me off but that fades when I realize she's oblivious to how fucking beautiful she is. She has no idea the amount of attention she's gaining because her only focus is making her way over to us. Fuck I'm lucky I met her when I did. It was only a matter of time before someone else made a move and stole my girl out from under me.

I chuckle as Bella approaches, her hands waving around as she animatedly talks on her phone. A minute later she disconnects the call and lets me know that Paige will meet me at my house Tuesday afternoon.

"You come with her if you can, Bella. I want you there, babe." According to what she told me at Casa Rosa, when she divorced her husband there were very strict guidelines drawn up regarding their children. I will gladly accept any advice she and Paige can offer because I know the war I'm waging with Charity is going to get messy.

"I have to drop the kids off at school at 7:10, but I will be free the rest of the day if their father picks them up like he's supposed to. If not, you'll have me until 2:45," she says. I'm so grateful she's willing to be in my corner while I go through this shit with Charity. She didn't sign up for this but she's a good woman for weathering the storm with me.

Bella offers to drop AJ off at my house since he isn't able to ride on my bike and safely hold on to me. I don't know what I would do without her. I give her a quick kiss in thanks and walk them to her vehicle. She follows behind as we make our way across town to my house. When we get there, she idles at the curb as I park my bike AJ hops out of her truck, going straight inside.

"Thank you for everything, Bella. I'm so grateful you were there today," I say walking over to her window that she's rolled down.

"It's my job, D. It was no trouble and in case you haven't noticed, I care about you both. I'll do whatever I can to help."

"Fuck babe. You're too good to be true. Have I told you how perfect you are lately?" I ask as I lean in to steal another kiss before she has to leave and pick up her kids.

"Drive safe Babe, and text me when you guys get home so I know you made it home okay."

"I will. See ya Tuesday, Diesel," she says before rolling up her window. As soon as she starts to pull away I realize that I want nothing more than for her to stay.

10

♡ Bella ♡

By the time Tuesday morning rolls around things are hectic like they usually are. I get Sophia ready for school while trying to feed them both breakfast. It's a miracle but we manage to avoid any major spills that would result in a wardrobe change. The real test is trying to track down Sophia's backpack. The girl would lose her head if it wasn't attached. She hasn't seen it since last Friday when she got home from school. Purple straps peeking out from under the couch catch my attention after ten minutes of scrambling around the house. With her bag rescued, we're out the door and headed across town to her elementary school. For once we just might make it on time.

I debate taking Luke to daycare, but ultimately decide I don't want to mess up his schedule. Trevor is supposed to get the kids tonight since his family is having a big party for his mother's 60th birthday. It's all for show of course, he just wants to look like the doting father, which he most certainly isn't. This is the downside of co-parenting. I hate them going back so soon since they were just there for the entire weekend. I shake it off because I don't want to be the mom who keeps her kids from their dad.

After dropping Sophia off at school, I take my baby to daycare and head home. I spend the morning getting the house back in order before hopping in the shower. I spend a little extra time pampering myself since I don't usually get the chance.

Before heading to Diesel's, I call and place a to-go order at Casa Rosa's for lunch. I know what everyone likes except for AJ, who's still home on bedrest for another day. After being told my order will be ready in twenty minutes, I gather up my things and drive across town to pick up our food.

I pull up to Diesel's house a few minutes before noon. As I'm parking, Paige pulls up waving and smiling through her window.

"Hey, pretty lady," I call to her as I'm opening the passenger door and pulling the food from the backseat.

"Hey yourself, Mamacita," she yells back, making me giggle. She refuses to stop calling me that.

"Please tell me that is a taco salad from Casa Rosa's with my name on it."

"It's a taco salad just the way you like it, with your name all over it." I can't help but laugh at her dramatics.

"Come on, let's go eat and see what advice you can give Diesel," I call over my shoulder as we approach the door. We barely make it onto the porch before it's swinging open and there stands D in a faded pair of jeans and a black ball cap he has on backward. He has no shirt, no socks, and no shoes. Bare-chested and barefoot, the man is a sight to behold. My mouth waters as I scan his body from top to bottom. This image should be added as the 8th wonder of the world.

"Afternoon. Need some help with that?" Diesel asks, already reaching for the bags in my hand.

"Hey, handsome. If you've lost your shirt, I'm hoping that you never find it," I say teasingly, with a smirk. I honestly missed seeing him yesterday. We texted a few times, but having our kids to contend with makes it more difficult to communicate.

Shaking his head at my teasing, he grins as he slides his hand behind my neck and pulls me into his chest. I wrap my arms around his back as he presses the sweetest kiss on my lips.

"Missed you, baby," he growls against my mouth.

"So, it's like that now, huh? Good for ya'll. At least someone is getting some action," Paige says. My cheeks warm with embarrassment at losing myself in the bubble that always forms when he's near.

"It's definitely like that now," D rumbles, not ashamed at all that someone was watching him kiss me. I honestly wouldn't have pegged him for public displays of affection, but I like that he is.

"Whatever you brought smells good, babe. But you didn't have to do that," he says as he takes the bags from my hands. Paige and I make our way into his house when he nods for us to follow him.

"I got your usual, handsome but I didn't know what AJ would eat so I ordered a couple of different things. Hopefully, he'll like at least something in that bag," I tell him, pointing to the bag he's rummaging through.

"He will literally eat anything, baby. He's an endless pit and he isn't picky at all." Well, that makes me feel better.

D leads us through his large living room and into a huge kitchen that opens up into an even bigger family room. This must be where they actually hang out. There's a black leather sectional sofa and the biggest television I've ever seen mounted on the wall. His house is fantastic but could use a woman's touch. The decorating is minimal and I can definitely tell it's a bachelor's pad.

Diesel sets everything on the table before taking off to get AJ to come and eat. When my stomach begins to loudly growl, I start getting our food out of the bag. I hand Paige her taco salad and a package of plastic silverware. The next two containers belong to D and me and the other three containers are for AJ.

As I'm sitting down next to Paige there's a knock at D's front door. A few moments later, a man who has to be D's father comes in behind my boys. *My boys?* Where did that thought come from?

"Ladies, this is my dad, Damon. I told him about everything that happened the other night and he wanted to be here today," he tells us while watching his dad stare down Paige. He lifts his brows at his father in question but the man has yet to take his eyes off her. She isn't doing much better and I giggle when she licks her lips as she gawks at him. Paige has always had a thing for older men. I don't think she's ever even dated anyone that was even close to the same age as her. Hmm, this could get interesting.

Clearing his throat to get his father's attention, he says, "Dad, this is my woman, Bella." *His woman?* Oh god, I really like that he thinks of me as his woman. It's crazy how much the simple statement excites me and sends tingles coursing through my body.

"And this is her cousin, Paige. She lives above our shop and is a law student over at Tulane University." I can't believe he remembered me telling him that. I'm surprised that he was actually paying attention when we talked that night at Rosa's.

"Damon, would you like to join us for lunch?" Paige asks with a flirty smirk on her face. Oh lord, I think she's found her next conquest.

"Don't mind if I do, Kitten." My brows shoot to my hairline as I look at Diesel in horror. Is this really happening? Don't get me wrong, the man is handsome just like his son and he doesn't look old enough to be D's dad, but he has to be almost fifty and Paige is only twenty-four. They can't seriously be attracted to each other, can they? Sitting down next to me, D leans over and whispers into my ear, "Not our business, baby." I know he's right but even he has to admit that it's a little weird.

AJ shakes his head at his grandpa as he takes one of the tins from the center of the table and moves into the family room to eat his lunch. I decide to ignore the sexual tension surging between my cousin and D's dad and tuck into my Chimichanga. AJ yells from his spot on the couch that his food was really good and thanks me for bringing it and my heart warms at how sweet he is.

"You're more than welcome, sweetheart," I yell back.

"Since he's entertained let me fill you in on the backstory, as well as what happened Sunday evening that landed AJ in the ER," Diesel says, before spending the next 45 minutes bringing Paige up to speed.

"I'm going to give you my honest opinion but I have to warn you. You may not like some of what I have to say. I want you to be prepared for that," she tells Diesel. Damon surprises me when he moves in to offer Paige his support. That's actually really sweet.

"I understand and wholeheartedly believe you when you say that Charity is a shitty and neglectful mother. However, proving it in court is another thing altogether. Unless you have documented incidents or have medical records that can show a history of accident or injury while under her care. It's a game of he-said, she-said. Do you have witnesses that have seen her being neglectful? Because hearsay won't hold up in court. From what you've said, she can spin the details of what happened Sunday. She could say that AJ instigated the fight and then ran and fell when he was trying to avoid punishment. This Matt guy can say AJ fell when he went to grab him and that he didn't push. Again, this all falls into the he-said, she-said category. AJ's back was turned away from Matt, so he can't be sure he was in fact pushed from behind. Although I believe him, being able to prove that in court is another thing entirely. I know this isn't what you're wanting to hear but the burden of proof falls on you," Paige tells him. I hate that it's going to be much harder than we'd thought but I'm so proud of Paige. Listening to her speak and hearing all that she's learned there's no way she won't be a kickass lawyer when she graduates. Damon has a look on his face that is pure appreciation and wonder at her awesomeness.

"Another thing, what is AJ's life like with his mother? Does she work or is she a stay-at-home mom who can say she's always around to supervise AJ? That goes a long way in court. Also, what do you do with him on the nights he's with you? If you obtain full custody, who will supervise AJ while you work? Sometimes, in cases like these, a home visit will be required to ensure the child is going to be in a stable home. The courts don't like shuffling kids from one unstable dump to another. They give custody to single fathers all the time, but believe it or not, they always look favorably on a complete family unit in the home. I'm not saying that a woman in the house makes a home safer or better, but we're going off of precedent here and that's what a lot of the guidelines are based upon," she tells him.

"Let me get this straight. You're saying that since I can't prove shit my chances at gaining full custody are slim," Diesel says, his voice laced with disappointment.

"That isn't what I'm saying at all. I'm just saying it isn't going to be easy. It's going to be really tough. But I have a suggestion and it involves the both of you," she says, swinging her eyes between me and D.

"Now hear me out before you guys start losing your shit. Okay?" she says gaining a nod from us both. I'm confused what she thinks we're going to lose our shit about.

"You need a wife. A wife will strengthen your chances of gaining full custody of AJ. Bella is an esteemed Critical Care nurse in one of the city's top hospitals. She's also the mother of two children of her own. She would look great on paper as your son's stepmother."

"Have you lost your damn mind? We haven't even been on a proper date yet and you're trying to marry us?" I ask her as I turn and look at D with wide eyes.

Good grief, he looks like he's seriously thinking about this. Has he lost his mind?

"Diesel, you can't be taking this seriously. We like each other, but you just said it yourself. This thing between us needs time and care devoted to it so we don't mess it up. I don't want to ruin this thing between us. I really like you," I whisper. The thought of ruining our chance before we even know what "this" is, honestly makes me want to cry. I don't want to lose him and AJ because we rushed into something we aren't ready for yet, and it's not just us that will be affected. We have the kids to think about too. What happens when they get attached to each other and then we end up not working out? They would be crushed. This is all too much, too fast.

"Bella, calm down. It's just on paper. You guys can get the whole thing annulled in a few months when this custody battle is over. Plus, you guys are about to be homeless in six days. This solves two problems and when it's over, I will personally file the papers for you guys," Paige says, trying to calm me down.

"Baby, why didn't you tell me you didn't have anywhere to go once you close on your house?" Well crap, Paige just had to open her mouth. I didn't want him to worry when his focus should be on AJ.

"D, we just met. I think I have laid enough of my baggage at your feet already. I wasn't trying to scare you away."

"Nothing is going to scare me away, Bella. I won't let it. Paige is right, it will solve two of our problems. It won't change how I feel about you if we do this or we don't. I still want to know everything about you and I'll do whatever it takes to make this work. Let's do it! We can decide what we want to do after the court case. This will give us more time together to get to know each other too. Apart, our lives are crazy but together we can do this thing, Bella."

"Okay! I'll do this with you but you have to promise me you won't leave me swinging out in the wind, D. I have my kids to think about too. I'm trusting you to do right by me. By us. Once AJ's case is settled, we'll sit down and evaluate what we want to do next," I agree, deciding to take this leap of faith with him.

"I will never let you down, baby," he says with a sweet smile on his face. The conviction in his voice eases a little of the tension this conversation has caused me.

"I'll watch the kids; you guys run down to the courthouse and get the process started now. The sooner the better," Paige tells us.

"Now?" I screech, and just like that, the tension is back plus some.

"Now, woman!" Paige insists. Shit, I thought I would at least have some time to process this. At this rate, I might stroke out.

"We'll go down there tomorrow, babe. We don't have to do it today. I don't even have a ring to give you," D says.

"Are ya'll really going to get married? You just met her. No offense Bella, but seriously, you just met him," AJ yells from the family room.

"Even the eleven-year-old has more sense than we do," I groan, the panic starting to rise. Is this a mistake? Normal people don't get married on a whim like this. Right? Especially two people who have already gone through a divorce because they got married too fast and too young.

Looking up at the clock, I see that it's almost time for school to dismiss.

"I have to call Trevor and make sure he's picking up the kids like he said he would," I tell the table. Standing up, I grab my phone from my purse on the bar and dial Trevor's number as I make my way to the front room. Trevor confirms he's picking them up but I say nothing about D and me getting married. I'm not ready to tackle that issue right now. Instead, I quickly end the call once I know my kids will be taken care of. When I turn around Diesel is leaning against the door frame watching me. He must have followed me in here thinking I was going to make a run for it while nobody was paying attention. As tempting as that is, I won't let him down when he seems to need me most. That's not the kind of woman I am.

"Thank you, baby. I know this is asking a whole hell of a lot from you." I can tell he hates needing help. We haven't known each other long but I can tell that he's the strong and silent type that's used to handling everything on his own.

"I know this whole thing is crazy, but it also feels like it's meant to be," he says pushing off the doorway and coming towards me. Once he's close enough, he pulls me into a bear hug. It's at this moment that I realize just how much I need his comfort.

"As crazy as I feel at this second. I think so too. I don't know about marriage and merging our families within a couple of weeks of knowing each other, But this... us, feels right to me too," I say leaning heavily into his chest and enjoying how it feels to have his strong arms wrapped around me.

D tilts my head so he can brush his lips against mine. Swiping his tongue across the seam, he asks for entry and I open for him. Delicately, he glides his tongue across mine in a slow wet kiss that's full of so much promise. His hands slide down my sides, and over my hips where he grabs my thighs to hoist me up. Revealing his strength, he effortlessly moves me and never once breaks our kiss. I wrap my arms and legs around him as he moves us. I moan when he presses me against the wall and grinds against me. Good grief I wish we were alone right now.

He groans, hesitantly pulling back and burying his face in my neck. I grin when he whispers how we have to stop before he has to have me here and now. All too soon, he's pulling my legs from his hips and setting me back on my feet.

"Soon, baby. The next time I fuck you, you'll be my wife," he says before placing another quick kiss on my lips.

I can honestly say the prospect of sleeping with him as my husband sounds perfect. Good grief, are we really going to do this? It's crazy, right? Certifiably crazy.

11

Diesel

"Just got off the phone with Trevor. He's keeping the kids for the rest of the week since his whole family is driving over to Gulf Shores. They're going to spend the rest of the week there to celebrate his mother's birthday. I guess they decided an impromptu family vacation was in order. He'll be there for a few days with the kids but his parents are going to bring them home since they're going to have all the grandkids for the rest of the time they're down there. I don't know how I feel about him not being there the whole time with the kids. Sophia was excited to spend time with her Grammy and Grampa though which made it impossible to tell her no," Bella tells me over the phone.

Checking the clock on the microwave, I see that it's only 6:00.

"I'm sure they'll be just fine, baby. Tell me where your head's at about tomorrow."

"I'm actually not freaking out anymore. Sure, this is all insane, but I figure at the very least it will only be for a few months until everything is settled with AJ's custody battle."

"And at the very best?" The more I've thought about it, the more I think we have a shot at making something lasting and real. This thing between us could last. There's been this undeniable chemistry between us since the night we walked into Casa Rosa together. We spent three hours getting to know each other and everything about us just clicks. We fit. Not to mention the fact that we're combustible in bed. Yeah, it's fast, but I always trust my gut and my gut is saying she's meant to be mine.

"This could all work out and be something amazing and beautiful," she whispers. It'll work out. I can feel it, down to my bones and soul deep.

"That's my girl. I want this too, Bella. I don't know why you were thrown into my life, but I know you're meant to be right here with me."

"Why is it, that you being so sure about this, makes it easier for me to agree with jumping on board?" she asks.

"I was thinking I could pick you up around 9:30 in the morning and we'll go get our rings. Then we can head down to the Clerk's Office for the marriage license and from there we'll go over to City Hall and get married. What do you think?" I shouldn't be in such a rush but admittedly I feel an urgency in case she starts having doubts and changes her mind.

"Yeah, okay. That sounds like a good plan. Are you sure you want to marry me, Diesel?" She needs to stop doubting me. I have always been one to know exactly what I want and I always go for it, no holds barred. She doesn't know that about me yet. But she will.

"I'm going to be really honest with you, Bella, and hope like hell you don't think I'm a psycho. The moment I saw you, I thought you were the sexiest woman I'd ever laid eyes on. The night we spent together with our kids, I thought you were the best mother I'd ever met and I wished my son had that in his life." I continue now that I have her full attention.

"The night we had dinner together and spent hours talking, laughing, and sharing our history. I thought you were the perfect woman and I'd decided then and there that I was going to do whatever it took to make you mine. Not taking you home and fucking you was torture, but I knew you'd be worth the wait. You're way too good for someone like me, but I'm a selfish fuck and I want you. I'll do whatever it takes to deserve you. So yes, I want to marry you. Since I'm being honest here, I'd hoped that one day I'd get us to the point where I could put a ring on your finger. I just didn't expect it to be this soon. But if you want to do things differently. We can, baby. You can still move in here and we'll slow all this down and take our time. You're worth the wait," I tell her as I lay all my cards on the table. I don't hold anything back, hoping to show her that there's nothing to be scared of and no reason to doubt us. I get it though, she's unsure because who in their right fucking mind marries someone after only knowing them for a couple of weeks?

"That is the sweetest thing anyone's ever said to me. Since we're being honest with each other, I had similar thoughts. It's just that acting on them so soon is scary and a little crazy. I think I'm afraid because I really want to give us a shot. The thought of messing everything up is disheartening. You're the best man I've ever met, Alex Logan, and I don't want to lose that," she quietly confesses. This woman... I'm humbled she thinks so.

"We'll make it work, baby. Let's make a promise that we'll talk it out if things feel like they're going to shit. But honest to God, babe, I don't think that will happen. We work. I know you feel it too."

"I promise that we'll talk things out if they feel like they're going south. And I do feel it too," she says with more determination in her voice. She's quiet for a beat and then damn near bursts my eardrums when she starts happily screaming.

"OH MY GOD! I'M GETTING MARRIED TOMORROW!" Her change in mood brings a smile to my face and I have to admit that her new sense of enthusiasm is contagious. "Oh crap! Diesel! I have to find something to wear. I'll see you in the morning. I have to go." Without waiting for a reply, she hangs up.

Women.

Sliding my phone into my pocket, I look over at my dad who's been eavesdropping on my conversation with my fiancé. I've been patiently waiting for him to weigh in on what he thinks about all of this.

"Can't believe you're actually getting married again," he says in disbelief.

"Well, believe it."

"I don't mean nothing bad by it, son. I just honestly thought Charity had turned you off from ever getting married again. I get that this is a ruse to fool the courts into giving you full custody, but aren't you afraid things will go to shit?"

"Can I let you in on a little secret? I'd marry that woman tomorrow regardless of the other shit swirling around me. I may not be in love with her just yet, but I know I will. That woman is perfect for me, Dad. I know it down to my bones. Knew it damn near the first moment I met her. I can't explain it, but I just know," I tell him. He may not understand but I know Bella is meant to be mine for the rest of our lives. I don't give a shit what anyone else thinks about it either.

"She's a beautiful woman and she'll be lucky to have a good man like you for a husband, son."

"Thanks, Dad."

"Now, tell me about Paige. She's a looker. She's young, but an old soul from the little I got to talk to her."

"Dad, go easy with that one, okay? That's Bella's cousin and I don't want any drama in the family."

"She asked me out. Isn't that kind of weird for a young twenty-something woman to ask an old man like me out?" he asks, ignoring my warning altogether.

"According to Bella, she doesn't date men her own age. She's always been into 'mature men' and she doesn't like putting up with spoiled momma's boys.'" We both laugh because the girl is sassy and has an odd outlook on men.

"Interesting."

"Did you tell her you'd go out with her?" I'm genuinely curious if he'd go on a date with a woman that is more than half his age.

"Told her I'd think about it," he says with a cat that ate the canary grin on his face.

"Gonna make her the woman you come home to at night? Let her cook you a good meal and fuck you to sleep?" I ask, laughing at the words he was spewing not long ago.

"I'd let that woman fuck me to sleep morning, noon, and night, boy. Did you see the tits and ass on her?" And I'm officially done with this conversation.

"Okay. That's enough. Hearing you talk about women and their assets makes me wanna ralph. You're my dad and I may be a grown man, but it still grosses me out."

"I'm going to need to think about her proposition. She could be a lot of fun, being a stripper and all," he says wagging his brows.

"Dad! Enough! Go home with all that nonsense," I tell him. I leave him to his shit as I move into the family room to hang out with my boy for the rest of the night.

"Whatcha doing, kid?" I ask, sitting down next to AJ. He's been glued to some crap on TV all night.

"Watching these guys street race and compete to be the fastest in their state."

"Can we talk?"

"Umm, sure. Am I in trouble?"

"No, you're not in trouble. I just wanted to talk to you about everything. What do you think about me and Bella getting married? You cool with it?"

"Yeah, if she makes you happy, I'm cool with it, dad. Plus, she's nice and really pretty."

"That's true. She is very pretty, and she's very nice too."

"Will Sophia and Luke be my brother and sister if y'all get married?" he asks.

"They'll be your stepbrother and stepsister. But yes, they'll be your siblings by marriage. You okay with that?" Searching his face, I look for any clue that this isn't something that he's okay with. I want to make this work but my son comes first.

"Cool. I've always wanted a little brother or sister. I get both now." The smile on his face is genuine and he seems excited that he is going to be a big brother.

"We'll get married tomorrow at City Hall and then the three of them are going to be moving in here with us. Are you good with that too? It's a lot of change for you at once."

"I'm good with it, Dad. I like Sophia. She's funny even though she's a girl. And Luke is just a baby, but he'll get big like me soon enough. He really likes you and me. We can teach him all the stuff you've taught me. Plus, you like kissing Bella." He grins as he pretends to gag. I get it, the thought of your dad kissing a girl isn't something any man wants to think about.

"I won't gross you out like your Pop just did to me. But if any of this isn't okay with you, you just tell me, okay?" I need for him to know that his opinions and feelings matter to me.

"I will, but I'm cool with all of this, Dad. I swear."

"Ok. Love you, kid," I tell him and drop a kiss on the top of his head. He tries to shrug me off. I don't know when he started thinking that he's too big for his old man to love on him.

"Love you too, Dad," he tells me, zoning back into his show.

12

♥ Bella ♥

AT 9:30, I hear Diesel knocking on my door. I rush down the hall while trying to attach the back to my diamond stud earring. Finally getting it screwed on, I throw the door open. "Sorry, I'm running a little behind. Come on in. I just need ten more minutes," I tell him with a quick smile. As I go to turn back towards my bedroom, D grabs my wrist and halts my steps.

"Jesus, the back of that dress is just as fucking sexy as the front. Turn back around. Let me get a good look at you," he says as he twirls me around. He looks at me from the bottom of my nude peep toe stilettos to the top of the blush-pink, lace mini dress that hugs my body like a glove. My hair is blown out big and full, and I've done my make-up just a tad bit more dramatic for the occasion with a deep pink matte lipstick and blusher to match. I've lined my eyes with a soft brown liner and added a coating of mascara to make my blue eyes pop.

"Fuck, I can't believe I get to marry you today. You look beautiful, babe. This dress makes your legs look like they go on for miles. You're testing my control here, woman," D growls, causing my breath to catch and my heart to race.

"Go finish getting ready, Beauty. If you don't hurry we may not make it out of here at all." I quickly take off to my room and switch out my bag before adding a couple of thin gold bangles to my wrist. With a spritz of my perfume, I look myself over one more time in the mirror. I'm as ready as I'll ever be on such short notice.

My heels clicking on the tile announce me before I even round the corner of the hallway. I stop in my tracks at the mouth of the living room when I get my first good look at Diesel. It's not that he's standing by the fireplace looking at photos of my kids with a soft grin on his face. Although his interest in my children is so sweet. No, it's the way the man looks when he's dressed in a nice pair of brown shoes, dark loose-fit jeans, and a black button-down shirt. He's the sexiest thing I've seen in years. His hair and beard are immaculately groomed and styled to perfection. He says he can't believe he gets to marry me but I'm the one who can't believe I get to marry this guy. He's sex on a stick and everything about him is orgasm-inducing.

"You're looking at me like you wanna eat me, woman. While I'd love for you to do just that. We have a schedule to keep. I promise to make it up to you later though, baby." I shiver as that deep sexy southern voice of his makes promises I can't wait to cash in on. I barely contain the moan that is on the verge of slipping past my lips.

Words escape me so I nod my head, agreeing that he'd better make it up to me later. I don't think I can speak without begging him to take me to bed now. When he reaches his hand out for me I resume my trek into the living room and glide right into his strong arms.

"Ready to go get married?" I ask him, finally finding my voice.

"Yes. Wild horses couldn't keep me away from marrying you today," He tells me with so much conviction that I have no other option but to believe him. His solid belief that this is all going to work out no matter what, instantly has the last of my reservations slipping away. He's right, we can do this. We can make this work.

"Me too. Let's get out of here and make me Mrs. Logan, handsome."

"That's the best thing I've heard all day, baby," he mumbles, placing a tender kiss on my cheek. I have a feeling he's avoiding my lips because he doesn't want to wear my lipstick. I grin thinking that pink raspberry probably isn't his color as he leads us out the door.

After leaving the house, we stop at a custom jeweler in town and pick out matching wedding bands. Diesel insists on buying me an engagement ring, even though I keep telling him I won't be able to wear it at work. He's not taking no for an answer and nothing I say can stop him. We leave the store with a 2.5-carat cushion cut halo engagement ring, and two white gold wedding bands. I don't even want to know how much all of this costs.

Our next stop is the circuit clerk's office to get a marriage license. Thankfully there is no waiting period required to get married in our town. Forty minutes later we walk across the street to the courthouse and wait in line to be married by the licensed notary that officiates marriages. When it's our turn, the man shows us where to stand so we're facing each other and begins reading from his wedding script.

"Repeat after me," he instructs Diesel when it's time to recite our vows.

"I, Alexander take you, Isabella, to be my wife. I promise to be true to you in good times and in bad, in sickness and in health. I will love you and honor you all the days of my life."

Tears are streaming down my cheeks as he professes a love that isn't even true to me. But I accept it as the gift that it is because I believe that love can grow between us. When prompted, I repeat the vows that I intend to keep.

"I, Isabella take you, Alexander, to be my husband. I promise to be true to you in good times and in bad, in sickness and in health. I will love you and honor you all the days of my life."

To my surprise, a tear slips from D's eye. He quickly brushes it away, and the smile on his face tells me he's overjoyed at us being husband and wife.

"By the power granted to me by the state of Mississippi, I now pronounce you husband and wife. You may kiss your bride," our officiant says with a smile on his face. He has the best job, getting to share in people's joy every day.

With those words, Diesel wraps an arm around my waist and pulls my body into his. Staring intently into my eyes, he slowly lowers his head and places his mouth on mine. As usual, we get lost in the moment as a growl is pulled from his chest and he thrusts his tongue into my mouth. We share a heated kiss that is full of passion and the promise of what's to come.

When we pull apart, both of us are breathing heaving with hooded eyes. The officiant clears his throat as he tries to contain his laughter. He motions us to a side table to finish signing all the documentation that will be filed with the courts, claiming that we are legally husband and wife.

"My wife," D whispers in disbelief as he watches me sign my new name on the last piece document.

"Too late to change your mind now," I say teasingly.

"Never. I will never change my mind, Bella. I want you to really hear me when I say that. You're mine now, and I'm yours. This is it, us, for the long haul. You hear me, baby?" He tells me.

"Yes," I tell him firmly, so he knows I really am hearing what he says and that I believe every word he says. I am in this one thousand percent.

"Good. Now let's get the fuck out of here. I need to take you home and get this dress off of you," he says excitedly as he rubs his hands together like a kid on Christmas day. His excitement makes me laugh at how truly eager he is.

"That sounds like a perfect idea, husband." As the title leaves my mouth, he groans in appreciation, and admittedly, I like the sound of it too.

Unfortunately, we were unable to go straight home and jump into bed together like we both desperately want. Our friends and family had banded together to throw us a small wedding reception and there was no way we could blow them off. Even though we desperately wanted to. Diesel has been complaining for two hours and keeps saying that he's in serious distress that only his nurse wife can cure and that if he has to wait much longer he may die. While he's being very dramatic; I kind of like that my new husband wants me as much as he does and has no qualms about voicing it to everyone.

I've gotten to meet the guys he works with and they're nothing like I thought they'd be. Since Crow is retired military, he was able to get the veterans lodge to let us use their banquet room for a few hours at no charge. I thought that was really nice that he did this for us. I'm pretty sure most of this shindig was Paige's idea. She must have enlisted Damon to get Diesel's buddies in on it. AJ, unfortunately, isn't here with us, having opted to spend the night with his best buddy tonight instead.

D's boss, King, invited his sister to come along and Paige and I have been talking with her since we got here. Paisley is absolutely amazing. Not only is she a sweetheart; she's also beautiful. The woman looks like a runway model. Paisley's full of sass, but with the softest and sweetest voice. I can imagine Sophia being a lot like her when she becomes a woman. Beautiful, but with a quiet sass that nobody expects.

She's been keeping tabs on Crow, the whole time we've been talking to her. She's constantly clocking his location in the room and I remember D saying something about her, King, and Crow all growing up together in foster care. I'm certain he said only King and Paisley were blood relatives but that the three were like siblings. She's not looking at him like a big brother. I'm not sure how this has gone unnoticed except for maybe it's something only another woman infatuated with a man would recognize. Make no mistake about it, she's interested in him, and with the way he's watching her, it's not one-sided.

I remember D's words from yesterday, *not my business.* When I look over at Paige, I see she's noticed it too. I subtly shake my head to not say anything. She nods in agreement, letting me know she reads me loud and clear.

We giggle when Damon stands on a chair and delivers a sweet toast in honor of his son and wishes us the best in our marriage and teases us by asking about more babies. Not happening, well, at least I don't think so. I wouldn't mind one more someday. Just not anytime soon.

Paige, not letting him outshine her duty as hostess, takes to a chair of her own. By the time she's done with her heartfelt words of love for me, Paisley and I are both a mess of tears and tissues. I pull her in a hug and thank her for always being here for me and having my back.

"I'm your ride-or-die bitch, Hells-bells," she says, making the whole room explode in laughter at her craziness.

"That you are, Paige-Poo." She's not wrong. She's been by my side for our whole lives. Not only is she my family, but she's also my best friend too.

Cake! Cake! Cake! Is chanted by everyone in the room and draws us to the banquet table. After cutting the cake, Diesel carefully places a morsel in my mouth before getting his own taste as he kisses me in front of all our friends and family.

"Ain't waiting much longer to get us out of here, babe," he says with his lips still firmly pressed to mine.

I reach for my small sliver of cake and hold it up for him to take a bite. He leans down, grabs my wrist to hold my hand still, and eats from my fingertips. Once he's finished chewing, he closes his lips over my fingers as he suggestively and slowly pulls them from his mouth. The naughty act causes my core to clench in anticipation. Damn, that's hot. Now I'm the one who's desperate to get out of here and be alone.

"Let's get out of here, Wife," he says through clenched teeth. Diesel obviously worked himself up with that move, too.

"Lead the way, Husband," I breathe.

We thank everyone for throwing this amazing party for us and say our goodbyes. Lacing his fingers through mine, D leads me out the door and rushes to get us home. Seems my husband is more than ready to consummate our marriage.

13

Diesel

PULLING into the driveway I put the truck in park and then just sit there. Staring at the front door.

"I know what I said, but we don't have to do this if you aren't ready, babe. I've thought about it the whole ride home and I don't want you to feel pressured to do anything you're not ready for." When I look over at her I find that she's staring right back at me with a sweet smile on her face.

"I don't feel pressured to do anything, Diesel. I want you because I choose you. Not because we got married today, and this is the normal expectation of what follows that. And in case you've forgotten, we've already slept together," she giggles.

I didn't realize how relieved I'd feel to hear her say those words. I know we've already slept together, but this feels bigger. More symbolic.

"Good babe. Good. Wait for me, and I'll come around and get you. Want to carry you across the threshold," I tell her, waggling my eyebrows and making her laugh as I get out.

When I get to her door, I scoop her out of her seat and hold her close to my chest bridal style, like she truly is today. I nudge her door closed with my hip and hurry towards the porch. When we get to the door, she reaches down and presses the code that unlocks the door so I can carry her across the threshold. My heart begins to pound against my chest as I carefully set her on her feet. This is really happening. I married this gorgeous creature today and she's my wife.

Turning back around, I pull her into my arms and just hold her for a moment. It feels like a dream that I never want to wake up from. Damn, how did I get so lucky? I make a silent vow to do everything in my power to make this thing between us unbreakable. After a beat, I grab her hand and lead her down the hall to our bedroom. Once we move her stuff in tomorrow, she'll feel more comfortable since she'll have her things around her.

Entering our room, I close and lock the door just in case Damon or AJ decides to come in and bother us. AJ is sleeping over at his buddy's house just up the street, but it isn't unheard of for him to come home and grab something he's forgotten.

Clearing my head, I take in my sexy wife from the top of her head to the tips of her shoes. "I don't even know where to start, baby. You look so fucking sexy in that dress. I can't decide where I want to put my hands on you first."

"I don't care where you start, as long as you start in the next thirty seconds," she says as her breath shudders.

Fuck yes. My girl is as ready for this as I am. Moving in behind her, I brush her hair out of my way to kiss the nape of her neck, occasionally running my teeth against the flesh. I grin as gooseflesh races across her exposed skin. Placing my hands on her hips, I pull her back into my chest and move my hands around to the front of her waist as I continue to kiss, suck, and nibble on her neck. She tastes like mine. The little whimpers slipping from her lips, only prove how much fun it's going to be to my time with her tonight. I was out of my mind with lust our first night together that I didn't take the time to savor every delectable inch of her body.

As I continue my assault on her fragile flesh, I'm in awe of how she freely gives herself to me. Her trust in me almost brings me to my knees. Placing one last kiss against her neck, I pull back and unhook the little clasp around her neck that's holding the top of her dress in place. Grabbing the little zipper that sits at her waist, I slide it down and almost swallow my tongue as I take in the line of her spine on her bare back.

"All night I kept wondering if you were wearing any undergarments," I rasp as my suspicions are confirmed.

"Hurry, honey," she moans, shifting her body restlessly.

I swallow hard as I caress the silky skin with the back of my hand. She's so damn soft. Picking up the pace, I press feather-soft kisses against her skin as I make my way down her body. Hitting my knees, I take in the goddess before me and groan in appreciation. I get to worship every inch of her. Lifting her legs one at a time, I take off her shoes and free her from the material pooled around her feet. Using my hands, I trace her long, lean legs and caress the globes of her ass that are exposed from the thong she's wearing.

Gorgeous. *My wife* is fucking gorgeous.

Rising from my spot at her feet, I remove my clothes before turning her around to face me. I scan every inch of my wife's beautiful body noting that she's truly a work of art. I say a quick thank you to the man above for taking his time when he created her.

Her tits sit high and firm, with the prettiest nipples I've ever seen. Leaning forward, I take one into my mouth and gently suck. Her head falls back on her shoulders as she moans in pleasure. I take in her every reaction, loving the way my wife responds to my touch. Gently biting down, I pull away allowing the bud to slide between my teeth. Taking the other in my mouth, I give it the same attention and get the same response. The sounds she's making are almost my undoing.

Looking up at her face, I find her lost in bliss with her eyes closed as she enjoys the feel of my mouth on her. I continue my assault as I make my way down her chest and to her navel, dipping my tongue inside, as I fall to my knees once again at her feet. For this woman, I would happily spend the rest of my life on my knees.

"Please," she moans as I slowly slide her panties down her legs. When she kicks them away, I get my first good look at her pussy. I find that she's bare, except for a small thin strip of hair. *Perfection.*

"Want your taste on my tongue, babe," I tell her as I lean forward and bury my nose between her thighs and breathe in her scent. She smells like lavender, with a hint of something sweet. Her head falls forward as I take the first swipe of my tongue along the seam of her pussy. With hooded eyes, she watches as I flick my tongue against her clit that's peeking from its hood. The taste of her honey explodes in my mouth and I groan in appreciation.

"Oh, God," she whimpers.

Pushing her thighs farther apart, I move one of her legs up and over my shoulder and dive back in. Using two fingers, I spread the lips of her pussy and pull her clit between my teeth, sucking the hard nub deep into my mouth. She tastes so sweet, like pure honey. Leaning forward, she digs her nails into my shoulders as she catches herself and holds on to support herself from falling.

"Yes. Oh god, yes," she wails, throwing back her head and moving her hips as she tries to ride my face.

I lick, suck, nibble, and eat at her, all while sliding two fingers deep inside her heat. I can feel her tighten around my digits as I fuck her with my fingers, stroking them back and forth until I find the spot that has her screaming out. She begs for reprieve but I continue to rub until she's shattering and coating my face with her juices. I gently suck on her clit, while slowly gliding my fingers inside her to ease her back down.

"Like that, baby? Like coming all over my face while I eat that sweet pussy?" I ask her, as I stroke my thumb along her sensitive clit.

"Yes. I love it," she pants, trying to pull away from my fingers that are still working inside her.

Gently removing my fingers, I climb to my feet and slam my lips against hers. She kisses me back, tasting her honey on my lips, as I pick her up and carry her to the bed.

Carefully, I lay her down and stare into her eyes as I climb between her thighs. Her body shivers as I notch my tip at her entrance and slowly begin working myself inside her an inch at a time.

"Fuck babe, your pussy's so tight. You feel so fucking good wrapped around me," I groan into her neck, trying to hold still and not come.

Once I've gained a semblance of control, I slowly start moving inside her and every thrust of my hips has her moaning and mewling. Pulling back, I latch onto her nipple and gently bite down while tilting my hips to hit that spot that drives her crazy.

"Oh god. Diesel. I'm going to come," she tells me as her pussy ripples around my hard dick.

"Not yet baby," I croak, slamming into her harder and harder wanting us to come together.

"Please, I need to," she cries.

"Not yet," I growl. At my denial, her pussy pulls me in deeper as I pick up my pace while thumbing lightly across her clit.

"Oh god. Yes! Right there," she tells me, letting me know that I'm hitting it right.

"Now baby," I demand, slamming into her once, twice, and then again before burying my dick as deep as I can as I come long and hard.

"Fuck! You feel so good, baby," I groan in ecstasy as she clamps down tightly around me. I kiss her for long minutes before finally coming up for air.

As I ease out of her perfect pussy, I freeze as my cum slide out from inside her. The sight has me thinking I wouldn't mind Bella round with my baby in her belly, but I know neither of us is ready for anything like that at the moment.

"Let's get in the shower and clean up so we don't make a mess of the sheets," she tells me.

Nodding, I climb out of bed, scoop her up into my arms, and carry her into the bathroom. I set her on the counter as I kick the water on, giving it a minute to heat up. Moving back over to Bella, I wedge my body between her thighs and pull her into my arms. I hold her close to me when she shivers from the air conditioning that's pumping through the house. I'm a big guy and am on the side of being hot-natured, so my air is constantly running. I keep it set at a cool sixty-seven degrees most of the year.

"Put your arms and legs around me and I'll carry you into the shower. We need to get you warmed back up and clean," I say, waiting for her to wrap her arms and legs around me. Once she does I move us into the shower and under the hot spray of water. Bella slides down my body and turns into the spray as she lets the water warm her up. My dick gets hard again as I watch the rivulets stream down her curves. My wife is so fucking sexy, I don't know how I'll get anything done with a constant hard-on from just looking at her.

"How'd I get so lucky to end up with a woman like you?" I ask her, voicing my thoughts.

"We're both lucky to have found each other, Diesel. It's not one-sided. Stop selling yourself short."

"Glad you think so, babe. I ain't seeing it that way, though. I hit the jackpot marrying a woman who is not only kind and sweet but is smoking fucking hot," I tell her truthfully.

"You're a goofball. I'm flattered you see me the way you

do, but I see the same thing when I look at you," she tells me with a warm smile.

I give her one more quick peck on the lips, and we get to work on cleaning ourselves up. It takes an astronomical amount of control not to take her again while we're in here, but I know that we have a long day ahead of us tomorrow.

Climbing out before her, I quickly dry off and throw on a pair of shorts before grabbing another towel and holding it open for her as she shuts off the shower. When she steps out, I wrap her in the towel and quickly work to dry her off so she doesn't get chilled again. Grabbing another towel, I watch as she wraps her hair in it and remember that her things are not here yet. I quickly grab one of my T-shirts for her to sleep in. As she slides my shirt over her head, I chuckle when it stops at the middle of her thighs. Bella is tall for a woman, so I'm not sure why I expected it to be a little longer on her.

"Sorry, baby. I don't have anything any longer."

"It's fine. I usually only sleep in panties and a tank, anyway. This covers a little more than my usual choice of pajamas."

I'd rather her sleep naked so I'd have easy access to her body, but with kids in the house, that's not exactly a viable option. When we go back into our bedroom, Bella picks up her clothes from the floor and lays them across the dresser before we both climb back into bed. I wrap my body around hers with my chest to her back and bury my nose in her neck.

"You good, Babe?"

"I'm good. Tired, but very good."

"Me too. Second best day of my life, aside from the day

AJ was born," I whisper into her neck, pulling her tighter against me.

"Me too, aside from my babies being born," she whispers back.

"Good night, baby. Sweet dreams."

"Night, handsome," she says with a yawn and within minutes she's fast asleep.

14

Bella

Everything slowly starts coming online in my mind as my eyes flutter open. With my head on Diesel's chest, my arm across his abs, and my leg thrown over his thigh, I realize I didn't move an inch all night. I'm shocked by this because I never gravitated toward Trevor in my sleep and I would have never been able to fall asleep like this with him. We both kept to our own sides of the bed, but looking over my shoulder, I'm clearly on his side of the bed. Interesting.

It shouldn't surprise me, though; I have felt a pull to D since the moment I met him, so it only makes sense that I would feel it in my sleep as well. Quietly extracting myself from around his body, I slide out of bed and make my way into the kitchen to start a pot of coffee. Sadly, I have to go back to work today and can't stay in our bubble any longer.

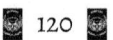

Diesel and I have been married for three days now, and it's been amazing. Complete and utter marital bliss. We've been in our happy little bubble and have barely come up for air. The day after our wedding, we went over to my old house and finished packing everything up. The next morning, the guys from Diesel's shop met us and helped bring everything over here, but unfortunately, they all had to work that afternoon. That left it up to me to put everything away myself. Thankfully, I'd spent the month before downsizing most of our things, so it didn't take me as long as it would have.

Diesel's house is so much bigger than I had originally thought. With five bedrooms, three baths, a living room, a family room, and the huge kitchen/dining room combo, there's plenty of room for our blended family. Another plus is that most of the spare bedrooms were empty and the guys were able to set up the kids' furniture before they left. Sophia and Luke's bedrooms look much the same as they had at our old place. I'm hoping that will help them adjust to their new home without too much stress.

It took the entirety of yesterday, working my fingers to the bone to get everything how and where I wanted it. I was so exhausted from moving that I fell asleep before my head even hit the pillows last night.

As soon as the coffee trickles into the pot, I open the fridge and see what we have that I can throw together for a quick breakfast. Grabbing the carton of eggs, the shredded cheese, and the fresh fruit I cut up yesterday, I decide to make cheese omelets with a side of fruit. With a plan in place, I fix myself a cup of coffee and get to work.

A set of arms that I've become very familiar with over the last couple of days wrap around me from behind as I'm standing at the stove. D traces his lips along the side of my neck as he murmurs, "Morning Babe. Sleep good?"

"Yeah. You?" I ask, leaning back into him.

"Sleep like the dead with you next to me."

Sliding the omelet onto a plate, I hand it over to Diesel and start the next one just as AJ comes into the kitchen. When I look over my shoulder at him, I can't help but giggle at his wild bedhead and rumpled sleep clothes.

"How'd you sleep AJ?" I ask him as I finish the next omelet and place it on the bar in front of him. Moving to the fridge, I grab a mini bottle of OJ and the bowl of fruit and set them in front of him too.

"Good," he mumbles around his fork while he shovels big bites into his mouth.

"Slow down and actually chew that, kid. You're going to choke, cramming all of that into your mouth at one time," D tells him wide-eyed making AJ grin.

"It's good. We don't usually get home-cooked food around here. I gotta eat it while I can," AJ says, laughing at the look his dad gives him. I'm thinking he may exaggerate a little for my benefit.

"Ok boys, finish eating so I can get this mess cleaned up before I have to leave for work."

"You cooked, Bella. We'll clean up the mess," Diesel tells me as he digs into his own breakfast.

"Thanks," I say appreciatively. I'm not used to someone cleaning up after I've cooked. Trevor never helped do the dishes. He just assumed it was my job to take care of everything around the house. I really need to stop comparing my man to my ex. They are worlds apart from each other and couldn't be any more different if they tried.

"Thanks for breakfast, Bella," AJ says, taking his plate to the sink.

"You're welcome, sweetie."

Diesel has done such a great job instilling good manners in his son. He is such a good kid and I couldn't be prouder of him. It's only been a few days of us all living together, but I've found that AJ likes to help with a lot of things. He helped me cook dinner last night and when there was nothing else for him to help with, he hung out in the kitchen with me while I finished what I needed to do. My heart breaks for him because all he wants is a mother's attention. His own mother should be the woman who gives it to him. I'm honored to be someone who gets to be there for him, but I know I can never take the place of his actual mother.

"Yeah, baby, thanks for cooking. It was great," D says, mimicking AJ's appreciation.

"It was my pleasure," I say, winking at them both.

"Are you wearing a wedding ring? What in the world?" Stacie asks loudly, as we're approaching the end of our shift. I've had it on all night, but she must have just noticed it since we haven't had a second to sit down all day. We have been really busy tonight, so I'm not surprised it took as long as it did for her to see it. It's not like it's a secret but I'm a little nervous about what she'll think about us getting married so quickly.

"Yeah. I am. Diesel and I got married a few days ago. I know it's really fast and crazy, but we're really happy. We get along so well, and everything about us just fits. He fits. He is nothing like Trevor, and I really want this to work," I rush to explain.

I know people in my life won't understand why I'd marry a man I just met, but I really am happy and I really want us to make this marriage work. I'm falling fast and hard for Diesel, and I hope he can get to a place where he loves me too. I'm pretty sure he's in just as deep as I am. Not to mention he treats me better than Trevor ever did.

"It is crazy, but crazier things have happened. If you're happy Bella, don't let anyone, even me, make you question the decision you've made. We get one go around in life. Just one. I say don't waste it. You did everything right with Trevor, and it still ended in heartbreak. Who's to say fast and crazy isn't exactly what you needed to find your soulmate? So, I'm happy if you're happy," Stacey says, giving me her sage advice that I hadn't realized how much I needed to hear. I'm so thankful for my friend. She's always been nothing but supportive.

"Thank you, Stacey. You're a good friend. I don't know what I'd do without you in my corner always cheering me on."

"That's what friends are for," she says as she hugs me tightly.

We spend the next hour getting the floor ready for shift change and getting patient charts caught up. As we're walking to our vehicles in the parking garage, I can see that someone is leaning against my driver's door, but I can't make out who it is. The second I round the back of my truck, I find Trevor.

"What are you doing here, Trevor?"

"We need to talk. I made a mistake, Bella."

"What? Made a mistake about what? What are you talking about?"

"Us. I made a mistake with us. I realize that now. I want to work things out, Bella. We were happy before I messed things up," he pleads.

"You've lost your mind, Trevor? You didn't just mess things up. You had sex with another woman while we were married. You were never home to help with anything, and that includes our children. We may have been married, but we hadn't had a marriage in a long time. I can see that now."

"I know. I'm sorry, Bella. Give me another chance. I can fix things. I know I can."

"Trevor," I sigh, "It's too late. I met someone and I'm married now."

"What? What the fuck do you mean you're married now? We've only been divorced a year. How could you marry someone else? How could you move on that fast?" he shouts at me.

"Two years, Trevor. We've been divorced for two years, not a year. And I don't answer to you. I don't have to get your permission to move on with my life. Where's Michelle, Trevor? Does she know you're here?" I ask him, and I don't miss the guilty look that crosses his face.

"We broke up yesterday," he mumbles.

"Ahhhh. I see now. Well, I don't care either way. I'm happy now. Truly happy. I have a partner who puts me and our kids first. He goes out of his way to do things to make all of our lives easier. I don't know what else to tell you. There's no going back after you did what you did to our family. Now, can you move please? I need to get home before my husband starts to worry about where I am," I tell him, completely done with this entire conversation. The nerve of this jerk thinking that he can just walk back into my life and pick up where we left off like he didn't throw our family away. As if he didn't dispose of us like we were nothing more than garbage to him.

Reaching out, he grabs my hands in his with a pleading look on his face. "Bella, sweetie, please just give me a chance to show you I can be different this time," He begs.

Yanking my hands out of his, I take a step back and look at him with fresh eyes. I never realized exactly just how manipulative and desperate he could be when we were married, but the blinders are no longer on.

"Go home, Trevor. I'm sorry, but there is nothing left between us. There never will be. I'm done with this conversation. If it doesn't pertain to our kids, then we don't have any reason to speak to each other. Please, try to respect that." He deflates when he sees the truth and determination on my face. Without another word, he ducks his head and walks away.

As soon as I get into my truck, I dial Diesel's number and connect the call to my truck. I click my seatbelt into place and start backing out of my parking spot just as he answers.

"Hey, baby. On your way home?" He asks, sounding sleepy. He has been trying to stay up until I get home on the nights that I work, but I can tell that he is running himself down.

"Yeah, I'm pulling out of the parking garage now. Um, Trevor was waiting for me when I came out from work tonight. He and Michelle apparently broke up yesterday. He thought he could come by and see if we could talk because he made a mistake. Can you believe him? As if the last two years hadn't happened at all."

"You okay? I know that couldn't have been an easy conversation for you."

"I'm fine. Actually, other than being annoyed he had the nerve to ambush me in the parking lot, I'm great. I told him I'm a happily married woman, and I wasn't interested in anything he had to say."

"Baby," he says softly and I can hear from the tone of his voice that he likes what I said. But it's the truth. We are happily married.

"Anyhow, I didn't need anything. I just wanted to let you know I'm on my way home and tell you why I was running behind. I should be there in about fifteen minutes."

"Okay. Drive safe and I'll see you soon."

"See you soon," I say and disconnect the call. I'm not sure what I did to deserve such a good man like my husband, but I'm sure glad he's mine.

15

Diesel

It's Sunday evening and Bella and AJ are in the kitchen icing a batch of cupcakes they baked earlier, while I sit on the couch watching the Miami game. As I'm listening to them laugh about something one of AJ's buddies did, I realize that this is what I had been missing in my life. Joy. Happiness.

I didn't even realize it could be like this and nothing could make this night any better except for Sophia and Luke coming home from their vacation with their grandparents. Which should be within the next half an hour.

Bella said their dad was with them for the first part of the trip, but I have a feeling his parents took up the brunt of the responsibility of keeping up with them. Which is fine, as long as they had a good time and were safe.

"AJ Logan! If you stick your finger in another swirl of icing, your behind will not get any cupcakes later," Bella laughingly scolds. I don't know who she thinks she's kidding with her threats. Even I know it's all lies and she's full of shit. My wife already loves our boy to death. They have been thick as thieves since she moved in.

"What? It was an accident Momma B," AJ whines to her. That's another new thing that he started doing yesterday and why I now think of my son as "our" boy. He's dubbed her Momma Bella, or Momma B for short. Bella cried when he asked her if it was okay to call her that. She told him he could call her whatever he was comfortable with as long as it "wasn't ugly". My woman is adorable and a true lady. She's pure class and hardly ever says a curse word. She has conditioned herself not to use profanity because she doesn't want the kids to repeat it. I've heard her slip once or twice but never in front of AJ and she has to be pretty upset. Like when she got home and told me everything about Trevor ambushing her at work. It brought up some unresolved anger, but I was more than happy to work that right out of her.

"AJ, do as you're told, son," I yell from my spot on the couch.

"Yes, Sir," he hollers back, understanding that I want him to mind what Bella says.

I get up from my spot on the couch when I hear the doorbell ring, and make my way through the kitchen and into the front living room. As soon as I swing the door open, Luke spots me and leans away from his father, reaching for me while he screams out, "Daddy!"

As the words leave Luke's mouth, I can see the anger spread across Trevor's face, but I ignore him and pull Luke into my arms.

"Hey buddy. Did you have fun?" I ask and he nods his head that he did.

"D, where's my momma? I gots to tell her 'bout my Grammy's birthday," Sophia asks, as she tries to pull her hand loose from her father's grip.

"She's in the kitchen making cupcakes with AJ, babygirl. Just holler once you go in and you'll find her."

"Cupcakes? They saved me some, I know it," she says as she tugs her hand away from Trevor's and rushes past me. I chuckle as she yells through the house for her mom. She doesn't even give Trevor a second glance, which just proves to me that he hasn't been a good father to his children.

"How are you doing, man? Thanks for bringing them home, my wife's been missing them like crazy," I say, trying to be civil but throwing a little dig in there that she's my wife now.

"Yeah. Sure. Give *Daddy* a hug, Lukie. I've gotta run," he says curtly. He emphasizes the word daddy, but Luke pulls closer to me trying to avoid his father. That's right, motherfucker, this is what you've done by ignoring your kids. I wish I had an ounce of remorse for this clown, but I don't and to be honest, I didn't cause Luke to feel this way about his father, so I have nothing to feel bad about. The title Dad is earned.

"He must be tired. Well, we'll see you in a couple of weekends when we drop them off for their visit," I say, backing up and shutting the door.

That was something else that Bella and I have recently talked about. I'm not telling Luke that he can't call me Daddy. He started that stuff on his own and if he needs that bond from me. It's his, no questions asked. We also decided that from now on we'll go together and drop the kids off so he doesn't pull any more shit with her. I may be a calm guy, but I won't take kindly to someone upsetting my wife.

"You want a cupcake, buddy? Momma made some," I ask, looking down at Luke as I make my way back into the kitchen.

"Yea," he says softly in his gentle little voice. Luke is the sweetest kid I've ever known. He has a gentle presence about him and I can imagine that when he grows into a man, that won't change. He'll be the kind of man that is calm and solid, that quiet strength that people gravitate towards.

As soon as I walk through the doorway, I take in my family. Sophia is sitting next to AJ at the bar and they're putting sprinkles on the cupcakes that Bella just finished icing. Bella's at the sink washing the dishes that she and AJ dirtied up and Luke is grinning at his sister's laughter. Everything about this picture is perfection. My kids are all laughing and happy, and my wife is the glue that holds it all together. I'm truly a lucky man.

I press a kiss to Bella's cheek as I walk past her. Placing Luke on the island in front of me, I grab him a cupcake and remove the liner before handing him the frosted treat. I laugh as he digs in, trying to shove the whole thing in his mouth. He's making a mess all over his face and clothes but it's nothing that can't be cleaned up easily when he's done.

"Sophia, did you eat one yet, or just jump in and start adding sprinkles?" I ask as I look at all the sprinkles that are scattered across the island that didn't quite make it onto the cupcakes.

"I gots' to make 'em pretty first, D," she huffs, sticking out her tongue in concentration. I barely suppress my own laughter when she drops a handful of rainbow sprinkles onto the cupcake that's in her hand.

"You're doing a great job, babygirl. They look beautiful," I tell her, making her smile at the praise.

As Bella scoots in next to me, I wrap my arm around her waist and pull her into my side as she smooches on her boy. Luke gives her a frosted-covered grin as she brushes his curls from his forehead and tells him and Sophia how much she's missed them.

I'm relieved that the kids seem okay being here. We talked to Sophia last night on the phone and explained as best as we could that they would live with me and AJ now and that we had gotten married. Sophia didn't seem to mind and was even excited to get to hang out with AJ every day. Luke is too little to know what is going on, but the boy doesn't seem like he would get into a fuss about much.

"What's for dinner, Momma? I'm hungry," Sophia asks.

"We're going to grill burgers and hot dogs tonight, sweetie. Momma made some of the pasta salad that you like to go with it. Does that sound good?" Bella asks, taking in the mess Sophia is making. She doesn't say a word about it, just smiles and enjoys watching her little girl do what kids do.

"The one with the little pepperonis?"

"Yep, the one with the little pepperonis. AJ was trying to eat them all, and I thought I was going to have to whoop him with my spoon, Sophia Grace. Can you believe that?" she says, teasing both Sophia and AJ.

"They were good, and I was hungry," AJ jokes.

"Baby, you want to stand here with him while I go fire up the grill?" I ask, looking down at her.

"Sure. Come here Luke, let's go get you cleaned up before dinner, honey," she says, as I hand him over. After pressing another kiss on my lips and I watch as she disappears down the hallway.

"You guys wanna come out here with me?" I ask, turning back around to look at AJ and Sophia.

"Yeah." Before I can even move, they're hopping off their stools and making a dash for the back door.

An hour later, we're all sitting out back enjoying the breeze and our dinner. Sunday dinners were apparently a weekly thing for Bella and the kids, so we decided it was something we were going to keep doing.

When I called and invited my dad, he declined until he found out Paige was going to be here tonight as well. Then he was all about Sunday family dinners and couldn't get here fast enough.

"Pop-Pop, will you push me on the swing?" Sophia asks, catching my dad off guard at her calling him that.

"I sure will, sweetheart, as soon as you eat two more bites of your hotdog like your momma asked you to do," he says. We all laugh at the pout she gives him. She thought she was going to get away with not having to do as her mother had asked, but her Pop is on to her.

"Did you tell your Pop thank you for getting the swing set, Soph? He's the one that got it and had the store come out and put it together for all of you guys," Paige says as she smiles at my dad like he hung the moon. She hasn't a clue how ornery the man is. He's eating up the attention she's showing him, which makes it even worse.

"At the very least, they're going to end up in bed together. I just know it. The sexual tension between those two is thick," Bella whispers into my shoulder.

"Not our business, Babe. I don't want us to get involved in their shit, and it affect our household. We're happy here and going to stay that way," I tell her. It's true; we don't need to get involved in their shit. They're both adults, but if it goes south, I don't want any tension between me and my wife over it.

"You're right. I don't want anything affecting our happy place either," she whispers, placing a kiss on my shoulder. For the next hour, we enjoy the cooler weather and watch the kids run around the yard and swing on the new swing set. I have to give my dad credit for buying it for them, and for thinking of Luke when he got a toddler swing to attach to the frame. AJ's been pushing him on it for a little bit and I love that they're already bonding. You'd never know these three kids hadn't been a part of each other's lives for long with how well they are together.

"We need to get them inside and ready for bed," I tell Bella, patting her thigh. She's been perched on my lap for the last hour with her face buried in the side of my neck. Slowly, she's been leaning more heavily into my chest so I know she's getting tired. When I turn to look at her I can tell she's running on fumes. I don't think she wants to break up the party but she can't stop yawning.

"Time for a bath and bed, guys," Bella yells across the yard at the kids as she climbs from my lap. She waves at our guests before herding our crew into the house.

"We're going to get out of your hair," Paige tells us as she gives everyone a hug. It's not lost on me that she and my dad are leaving at the same time. Bella swings her accusing eyes at me as if to say, "see I told you so".

"Come on, babe. Let's get these rugrats inside and ready for bed. I got something for you once they're asleep," I tell her, waggling my eyebrows suggestively.

An hour later, I deliver on my promise.

Twice.

16

Diesel

Pulling into the parking lot, I look over my shoulder and ask, "Y'all ready to build some sandcastles and play in the water?"

"Yeah!!!!" comes the kids excited cheers. We spent all of last night trying to decide what we could all do together today. It was a tie between the drive-in movie theater and the beach, so we flipped a coin and the beach won.

"Bella, you get the kids and I'll grab all our shit out of the back," I say, kissing the back of her hand that's laced in mine.

"Okay."

Hopping out of the truck, I walk around and open the back end and can't help but laugh at all the shit Bella has stuffed inside. If there's one thing that you can count on when it comes to my wife, it's that she is prepared for anything. A cut, a scrape, or the zombie apocalypse.

I sling the beach bags over my shoulder before grabbing the chairs, umbrella, and cooler. Once I have everything secured in my hands, I head for my family. Once they find the perfect spot, I start setting up camp. It takes me ten minutes to get put up to Bella and the kids' specifications. Once I'm done everyone is happy, which is all that matters to me.

Hefting myself down into my beach chair next to Bella, I watch as AJ and Luke dig a hole in the sand to contain the crabs that AJ plans to catch. He does this every time we come to the beach. He loves to set them all loose before we leave, so he can chase after them as they escape to the ocean. I can't wait to see Luke and Sophia's reaction when a few dozen crabs take off running for their life.

"Dad, come help us build a sandcastle," AJ hollers.

"Duty calls, big guy," Bella chuckles. I damn near swallow my tongue when I turn my head to comment back and find my smoking hot wife in an American Flag string bikini. I wasn't aware that's what she had on under her sundress, or I wouldn't have let her leave the house.

"Good God, woman. Are you trying to get all these men killed? Cover your sexy ass back up. This," I say, waving my hand at her mostly naked body, "is only for me to see." I quickly dig through one of her many bags and grab a towel to wrap around her. She has no idea how sexy she is and that it should be a crime to temp the male population.

"Stop being silly. I'm wearing more than most of the women here," she says, swatting my hands away.

"Not worried about the rest of them, only worried about what's mine." She laughs like I'm joking. I'm not. Every guy on this damn beach is drooling over her. I just saw one get smacked on the back of his head by his very pissed-off woman.

"Look mister," she says full of sass, pointing in my face and showing just who Sophia gets it from. "It doesn't matter who stares, drools, or catcalls. I'm going home with you and that's all that matters. There is no way I'm going to sit out here all day burning up. I want to get a tan and I can't do that if I'm covered up." She has valid points, but I still don't like it.

"You're right. Let's enjoy the beach with the kids," I say, giving her a quick kiss and deciding to pick my battles.

Moving to where the boys are armed with their shovels and pails, I sit down beside AJ and watch as Luke moves around him and climbs into my lap. "Let's build a giant sandcastle!" Sophia shouts as she wraps her arms around mine and AJ's necks and squeezes in between us.

"Let's do it." For the next two hours, we build castle walls and towers, while the boys dig a moat around the construction. Looking over my shoulder, I see Bella is still sound asleep in her chair. I noticed about twenty minutes into our build and have been doing my best to keep the kids entertained so she can sneak in a much-deserved nap. I swear the woman doesn't get enough rest.

Hearing the ice cream truck in the distance, I put my finger to my lips, and point to their momma. Standing, I lift Luke and grab Sophia's hand before telling AJ, "Grab that ten-dollar bill out of the pocket of that bag, bud."

Once he's grabbed the money, we make our way up the beach and to the edge of the grass to wait for the truck to make its way over to us.

"What are you going to get, Sophia?" I ask.

"A purple snow cone."

"I'm getting a red one," AJ says.

"What about you, Luke? What are you going to get?" I ask tickling his belly and making him giggle.

"Ice!" he squeals when Sophia and AJ get in on the action and tickle him too.

"Sophia, what does your momma usually get for him?"

"A Bomb Pop. It's her favorite and they share it." Good to know.

When the truck approaches I order what the kids want and we make our way back down to our spot in the sand.

"Momma's awake!" Sophia shouts and takes off running for her.

"Here ya go, babe," I say, handing her a Bomb Pop of her own.

"Aww, this is my favorite," she says smiling sweetly.

The rest of the day goes by quickly as we finish our castle while Bella takes a million pictures. I take the kids to the edge of the water and listen as they laugh and scream as it rolls across their toes.

"Ok, guys. It's time to pack up and head home. We still gotta make dinner and get everyone bathed before bedtime," Bella says, receiving a chorus of groans from the peanut gallery.

As I watch my kids trudge through the sand towards my smiling wife, I realize this was the perfect day.

Hanging up the phone, I try to process what I just heard. When Craig called asking me if I was still married to the hot woman that works in the ER, I should have known it would not be a pleasant conversation. Craig told me he saw my wife holding some man's hands in the ER parking deck and knew it was her because he had seen our wedding photo on my station. I'm trying not to lose my shit, but he said they looked awfully cozy. I should have known this shit would happen again. Can any woman stay faithful? I thought Bella would be different, but I guess I was wrong about her, too. Maybe we rushed things, and she wasn't over her ex like she claimed to be.

Deciding to handle this situation now, I pull my phone out and call Bella. She answers on the second ring.

"Hey handsome, I've been missing you. Will you be home soon?" she asks sweetly, but I'm not falling for the shit.

"Don't! Just fucking don't! Were you going to tell me you were holding that prick's hand? That you were cozied up to him outside of your work. Did you think you could play me and I wouldn't find out the truth? You shouldn't have married me if you weren't over that motherfucker. I can deal with a lot of shit, Bella, but we promised there would be no lying and hiding shit when we got married. Did our vows mean nothing to you? Is this just a game that you thought you could drag me and my son into? If you still want that bastard, then he's all yours," I seethe into the phone, no longer able to hold on to my temper.

"What are you talking about, D? I didn't do what you're claiming I've done. I don't want him. I told you that already."

"More fucking lies. Someone saw you, Bella. He called and told me what he saw. He doesn't even know you or have a reason to lie to me," I growl, so fucking pissed off that I let myself be blinded by the promise of her.

"Wait. Are you accusing me of something here? Have you lost your mind? Are you having regrets about getting married? Is that what this is about? I don't understand what you're implying, but I didn't do anything wrong. I swear to you, I didn't," she says, doubling down on her bullshit.

All the lies are just pissing me off more. I can't take this shit right now, so I hang up the phone before either of us says anything else we can't take back. I need to think about everything and decide what to do for my son and me moving forward. I just hope that can include Bella and the kids I have come to think of as my own. The thought of there being no more us has my chest clenching and my heart pounding. I thought things were going well. I never imagined I would ever feel anything but admiration for my wife, but that is the farthest thing from my mind and that doesn't sit right with me. Fuck. How did we get to this place where everything feels like it's falling apart and is going to implode with the slightest misstep from either of us? Filing for divorce so early in the game doesn't seem right either. I need to talk to her when I get home so we can figure this shit out.

For the next two hours, I wonder if maybe I jumped the gun when I called her without thinking through everything Craig told me. She told me that Trevor showed up at her work. She told me everything they said to each other and how he'd ambushed her. Maybe Craig misunderstood what he saw and she isn't lying to me at all. Trevor could have grabbed her hand. Fuck, I may have just let my past sabotage my future.

When I pull up to the house after a long night at work,

I get a bad feeling in my gut. The first sign of trouble is that the porch light isn't on like it usually is when Bella is home. She's made it a habit to leave it on for me when I have to work late. Pushing the button on the garage door opener, I wait for it to open and when it does my heart sinks. The second sign of trouble is that Bella's Tahoe isn't where it's been parked every night this week. Trying not to jump to conclusions, I pull inside and shut off my bike. Removing my helmet, I hang it from my handlebar. Pushing off my bike, I make my way into the mudroom where I'm greeted with nothing but darkness inside our house. I move throughout the kitchen and there isn't a trace of anyone being home. Making my way down the hall and into our bedroom, I find it empty, too. Looking around, I see that some of her things are missing. Shit, did she leave?

Picking up the phone, I scroll down my contacts and hit my dad's number. It rings and after long moments he finally picks up.

"Saw her leave an hour ago, son. I'm not sure what is going on, but the woman I watched leave your house is not the woman I have come to know over the last week. She was crying and took off before I could go over and find out what was going on. So, I'll ask you, what in the hell is going on?"

"We had a fight. One of my clients called and told me he saw Bella with her ex, but once I had a chance to digest what he told me, I think that I may have jumped to conclusions," I tell him, rubbing the back of my neck in embarrassment at just how badly I treated Bella.

"Let me give you some unsolicited advice. Don't let

whatever is going on fester. Find your woman, Alex, and fix your shit now," he tells me.

My dad has regrets about the way he left things before my mom took off when I was younger.

"I hear ya, old man. I'm going now. She's probably over at Paige's house. At least I hope that's where she went. Thanks for keeping an eye on the house," I tell him disconnecting the call. I'm glad that AJ stayed with his friend tonight so that I can track down my woman. I just hope that I didn't fuck things up too badly.

17

Bella

I'M EQUALLY furious as I am heartbroken when D hangs up the phone on me. I have never lied to him and wouldn't start now. No way am I sticking around to be accused of cheating and lying. I'm so thankful the kids aren't here right now. Slamming my phone down on the counter harder than necessary, I storm off to our room. No... his room, to pack my overnight bag with enough clothes to get me by for a few days until I can figure out where we'll go from here.

Once I've packed everything I'll need, I shut off all the lights and head out the door. Before I close the garage, I send a quick text to Paige telling her I'm coming over. She texts back to come on over since she's off tonight and doesn't have class in the morning.

By the time I pull up to her apartment and park next to her car, my face is stained with tears and I can hardly breathe. Paige is going to lose her shit... I mean crap when she sees me all torn up like this again over a man. What is wrong with me? Why can't I seem to get it right when it comes to relationships? Slowly, I walk up the steps and knock on the door. Wrapping my arms tightly around my middle, I wait for her to answer.

"Hey biot..." she trails off when she sees my face. "What's wrong and who am I killing?" she seethes as she opens the door wider, dragging me in behind her.

"D... he..." *hiccup*, "he called accusing me of, I don't know, lying and cheating on him with Trevor." *Hiccup*, "I didn't, though. I swear I didn't. I told him he showed up at my work trying to win me back." *Hiccup*, "I even told him everything we said to each other. The only thing I didn't tell him was that Trevor grabbed my hands, but honestly, it slipped my mind. I wasn't trying to hide it from him." Paige pulls me into a hug and rubs her hand up and down my back soothingly. When I finally calm down, she pulls back and swipes the tears from my face.

"Now that you've calmed down some, explain to me what happened," she tells me as she pulls me over to the couch to sit down.

"Wait, wait, wait! Hold that thought! From the look of you and what you've said so far, this is going to require a lot of wine," she says as she rushes off to the kitchen. In the blink of an eye, she's carefully gliding back into the room with two of the biggest wine glasses I've ever seen in my life. From the looks of them, they're filled to the rim. She also has two bottles tucked under her arms and a family-size bag of Twizzlers. I can always count on Paige to know just what I need when my world feels like it's falling apart.

Starting from the beginning, I run through everything that happened, from Trever showing up at work, to the phone call today with D. Before either of us realizes it, we've started on the second bottle.

"Men are so damn stupid," Paige says, as she pours us another glass. I giggle as she looks at the bottle accusingly like she can't quite understand where it all went. Her confusion makes my giggle turn into full-blown laughter. I didn't think it could happen with the state of my heart at the moment.

"They are," I agree, sipping my wine through my Twizzler like it's a straw. "The worst part was the way he spoke to me. Paige, I didn't think I would ever hear my husband talk to me the way he did today. Questioning what happened and what he heard is one thing, but being so vicious was uncalled for. He didn't even ask me what happened. He just jumped right into throwing accusations around. If he would have just given me a second to explain, I could have told him that I just forgot that Trevor had grabbed my hands and that I yanked them back immediately. Instead of having the courtesy to hear me out. He hung up on me," I tell her, slumping back in my seat and taking another healthy swig of my wine. "This is really good. What is it?"

"Boons Farm, the Strawberry Hill one. The cheap shit, but it tastes good," she says, trying to take a drink straight from the empty bottle. Good grief, I think we may be a little drunk.

"So, I have to ask. What's going on with you and Damon? You guys always seem to be chummy when we do Sunday dinners at the house." The thought of no more Sunday dinners with them makes my heart sink.

"I don't know. I mean, he's hot. I know he's older, but you know I have never been interested in guys that are my own age. They always want to play games, and I don't have any spare time in my life for that nonsense."

"That doesn't exactly answer my question though."

"He keeps blowing me off. I ask him to out and he keeps saying 'we'll see'. But you know how I am. I love a good challenge so for the moment, I'm chasing him I guess. I'm probably wasting my time. But I'm busy, so it's all in good fun for the time being," she explains and I guess that makes sense. I could actually see them being good together, but time will tell.

"Let's watch *How to Lose a Guy in 10 Days* and rag on men," Paige suggests, causing me to burst out laughing. This has always been her go-to movie when she's confused or pissed at the opposite sex.

"Nothing could be more perfect," I agree and for the next two hours, we laugh, cry, and drink entirely too much wine.

"All right, Hells-Bells. This girl is hitting the sack. I've had way too much wine and I don't think I can keep my eyes open another minute even if I wanted to," my drinking partner declares as the credits roll across the screen.

"Thanks for tonight, Paigie-poo. I can always count on you to have my back."

"Always, Bella. I always have your back," she murmurs as she stumbles from her spot and staggers down the hall to her bedroom. Leaning back on the couch, I start to make a list of what I need to do tomorrow when there's a knock on the door. Climbing to my feet, I hurry to answer it figuring it can only be one person.

18

Diesel

When I pull up to Paige's apartment, I'm instantly relieved to see Bella's Tahoe sitting next to the piece of shit Honda that Paige drives. Hopping off my bike, I tromp up the steps and knock, praying that one of them will open the door when they realize it's me on the other side of it.

My head thuds as I lean it against the door and I hate that my wife felt like she had to escape her own home because we had a fight. I know it's all my fault and I deserve whatever she dishes out. I shouldn't have said the things I said and I shouldn't have been so cruel about it either. I should have waited until I was off work so that we could sit down and talk things out, but when I heard Craig's interpretation of what he saw, it had me seeing red. I royally fucked up and I hope that I can smooth things over with Bella. I could kick my own ass for how I handled things. She deserves better from me and I'm ashamed that I let her down.

When I hear the lock turning, I step back from the door and what I see has my heart plummeting into my stomach.

My beautiful wife looks completely wrecked. Her eyes are puffy and the tear tracks on her cheeks tell me she's been crying. Fuck! I promised myself that I'd never be the man who made her cry.

"I'm so sorry, baby. Please forgive me. I fucked up and I know it."

"You were so unfair, Diesel. You didn't even give me a chance to wrap my head around what you were saying, much less a second to defend myself," she quietly sobs. I reach for her and when she pulls away from me, I feel genuine fear for the first time in my life. Lowering my head in shame, I pour my heart out. I don't care if it makes me look like a pussy. I can't lose my wife.

"I was. You're right. It was unfair, and I'll never be able to tell you how sorry I am that I jumped to conclusions. I should have waited to talk to you when I got home so we could figure out what was what. I just went off experience and I know that isn't fair to you. You're not Charity and it's not okay to punish you for her sins. Please forgive me Bella and let me make it up to you. I swear, baby. I will never hurt you again. When I came home and you were gone, I knew I had to move fast to fix things. Please, baby. Please tell me it isn't too late to make things right between us. Can you forgive me?" I plead.

She continues to cry and I can't take it anymore. I press my hand into her belly, pushing her back inside the apartment and following behind her as I do. I quickly close the door before pulling her into my arms and holding her as she lets out her emotions. I tighten my hold, pulling her into me even closer, and wish that I could undo this whole day and do things differently.

Pressing my face into her hair, I tell her how sorry I am and that it's going to be okay. I whisper for her to let it all out, vowing that I won't ever give her a reason to cry again. After she's worn herself out, I bend down and lift her into my arms as I try to remember where Paige's couch is. Sitting down with Bella in my arms, I rock her like a child and try to give her as much comfort as I can. I make a promise to the man upstairs that if he can help my woman find it in her heart to give me another chance, I will never make her cry again. I vow to spend the rest of my life making her happy.

"I forgive you, but please don't hurt me again, D. I don't think my heart could survive it," she whispers into my chest.

"I won't. I swear on everything, Bella. I won't ever do anything to hurt you again. Where's your stuff, babe? I'm taking you home where you belong."

"I never got it out of my truck," she says, lifting her face and looking at me. I feel like such a bastard for causing her to be in the state she's in.

"Where are your keys? I'll drive us home and come back for my bike tomorrow."

"I can drive myself so you don't have to leave your bike, D."

"You're in no shape to drive, Bella. Come on, let's go home," With her still in my arms, I grab her keys from the bar when she points them out, and carry her out the door to take her home. She nods off as soon as I pull out of the parking lot and my chest tightens as she continues to whimper in her sleep. Never again will I jump to conclusions, the price is just too heavy and my poor wife is the one who is paying for it. I quickly get us home and put her to bed. I'm reminded how perfect my wife is when she calmly explains everything and forgives me for being an asshole. I hope that tomorrow will be brighter for us both.

The next morning, I'm not surprised that I wake before Bella. The events of last night flash in my mind and I know she can use the extra sleep, especially after what I put her through. Climbing out of bed as quietly as I can, I go into the kitchen to start a pot of coffee. Wanting to do something nice for her, I start making breakfast so I can bring it to her in bed. I come up with a plan to spend the day pampering her and reminding her how I feel about her. Once we got home last night, she explained to me that Trevor had grabbed her hands when he was trying to plead his case, but she didn't allow him to continue. She never even thought to mention him grabbing her hands because she was so pissed off by the things he said and how he couldn't see that he'd done more than he was owning up to. I felt like a fool for ever doubting her. She isn't the kind of woman who would step out on her man. I know this about her, but I let my experiences with Charity cloud my judgment. We were up for hours talking everything out and thankfully my girl had the grace to give me another chance after I made the biggest mistake of my life.

I grab everything I need from the fridge and get to work making her some French toast that she can enjoy in bed.

19

Bella

"Hey Stacie, can you hand me Mr. Johnson's chart, please?" I've been trying to get a little bit ahead so we aren't here any longer than we need to be. It's been absolutely insane in our emergency room tonight. There's a full moon and something about that always has people out of sorts.

"Here you go, Bella," she says as she hands it across the counter to me. Just as I set the file down, our CNO yells out that we have a bus en route. The patient is a female, twenty-nine, code blue. That means our incoming patient is in cardiac or respiratory arrest and it's all hands on deck. Our unit flies into action as we work in sync to make sure the room is ready for our incoming patient.

Looking around, I can tell that everyone's adrenalin is flowing. In the next moment, the doors burst open and the paramedic is on top of our patient's body performing chest compressions as his partner steers the gurney into the room I direct him into. Together, we transfer both patient and the working paramedic onto the bed. He quickly hops off so

Stacie can take over, just as Dr. Toler comes barreling into the room, accessing the situation. I freeze for a brief second when I glance up at the patient's face. I'm shocked to find that it's AJ's mother but quickly get my head back in the game and do my damnedest to help save her life. Everything moves at a rapid pace as we work quickly to try and stabilize her.

The medics shout out the information they were able to gather at the scene and from what they're describing it's becoming glaringly clear that she's overdosed on opioid narcotics. Dr. Toler quickly administers Narcan, hoping it will counteract the poison she has put in her system. When we don't get a reaction, Dr. Toler puts the paddles on her chest. Her body jolts from the shock and thankfully, her heart starts beating and her vitals stabilize, even if still slightly elevated. Signs of life are always reassuring and give us hope things will turn around for the better. The activity in the room slows down slightly now that we're able to start a full workup.

With Charity now stable, I pull my CNO aside and give her a brief rundown of who Charity is to my husband and me. She pulls me from the case for my protection, as well as the hospitals. Liability is a tricky thing to maneuver around, but since we have plenty of critical care nurses on staff tonight, I'm not needed.

Two hours later, the toxicology report comes in and it's confirmed that Charity suffered from an overdose. She was basically poisoned since the methamphetamines were laced with fentanyl.

Charity was deprived of oxygen long enough that she is going to need months of rehab if not a permanent long-term care facility. It will all depend on how the next 72 hours go.

I don't know why Charity did this, but I don't think it was intentional. The fact she's using drugs does explain why she called D last night and asked for us to keep AJ another day. She clearly was on a bender and wasn't sober enough to take care of her son. At least she had the forethought to make sure he had a responsible parent watching over him. Diesel's right, she's selfish for how she treats AJ, and for being irresponsible when it comes to doing what it is best for her child.

We will definitely need to take this to Tinzley in the morning so she can petition the courts again for us. Sharing custody with this woman is unacceptable.

I feel like I'm between a rock and a hard place because of patient confidentiality. It's killing me not being able to call Diesel while I'm on shift and tell him what is going on. I don't know how we're going to tell AJ about any of this either. He may not want to live with his mother, but he's a sweet boy and would never want anything bad to happen to her. He loves her regardless of her being a terrible mother.

The next four hours drag by but as soon as my shift is over, I quickly grab my stuff from my locker and jog to my truck. Once I'm in, I click the locks and hit D's number on my phone. As soon as the call connects to my truck, I back out of my parking spot and head towards home. It rings a few times before he finally answers.

"Headed home, baby?" he rasps, sounding like I woke him. I glance at the clock and cringe when I see it's almost midnight. Shit, I should have just waited until daylight to tell him what was going on.

"I'm so sorry, honey. I didn't even think about the time. Go back to sleep. I'll be there in about ten minutes."

"What's wrong?" He already knows me so well.

"I have some bad news, sweetie. Charity came in as a patient tonight. It was really bad," I tell him before giving him the play-by-play of everything that happened when she was rushed through our doors tonight.

"Damn. All right. I'm getting up. We'll talk more when you get here and figure out what we need to do about the court stuff and how to tell AJ."

"Okay. I'll be there in just a few minutes."

"I'll see you soon. Drive safe. Love you, baby," he says, disconnecting the call and leaving me reeling. We haven't said the words, but we show each other love with our actions and he proves it with everything he does for me and my kids.

When I pull into our driveway, he's already headed toward my truck. I shut off the engine and grab my bag just as he's opening my door. Before he can say a word, I blurt out, "I love you, too."

He is stunned silent for a beat but quickly recovers as he tells me, "I know. You show us every day."

Diesel then relieves me of my bags and helps me out of my truck.

Clicking the locks over my shoulder, I let him guide us through the front door and down the hall to our bedroom. I kick off my shoes and make my way to our bathroom; needing a quick shower before we sit down to talk. Diesel comes into the bathroom and hops onto the counter as I put my dirty scrubs into the hamper. He doesn't say a word, just tracks my movements as I walk around the room naked.

"I don't know what we need to do about what happened tonight. Legally, I'm not supposed to give you information about a patient. Normally I wouldn't, but this situation was different," I tell him as I climb into the shower.

"I think we just need to not do anything." Is he out of his mind?

"We need to let it play out. When she doesn't show up tomorrow to pick up AJ, I'll call her phone. After that, we'll call the lawyer and tell her that Charity didn't show up. They will have to look into it and uncover everything that is going on right now. We're just going to resume our normal routine until she doesn't show up. That will protect AJ, that will protect you, and everything else will work itself out."

"Good idea." It could work and we'll get the same outcome. The only thing that matters is making sure that AJ is safe.

After a quick shower, I dry off and put on my sleep clothes before D and I climb into bed. It's been a long day for both of us and we're both exhausted.

"Thank you for trusting me enough to tell me about Charity when we both know that it could destroy your career. I won't make you regret giving me that trust, Bella."

"I know, and thank you for being someone I can trust. I can't describe how it feels to have someone in my corner who has my back."

"Always, babe. Always," he promises as he pulls me tighter into his chest.

"Goodnight, D. Love you," I mumble, half asleep already.

"Night, baby. Love you too." These are the last words I hear before everything fades to black.

It's been a few weeks since Charity came into my ER and almost died. We waited until that Monday evening and when she didn't show up, we called the police. Diesel tried to file a police report but was told that he had to wait twenty-four hours. The following morning, we called Tinsley, and she took it from there.

Thursday afternoon, we were shocked that Charity had signed over her rights completely. Something that we hadn't expected her to do. Her recovery was going to be a long uphill battle. The doctors informed her that she would probably never be the same. In the end, she did finally put her son's best interest first. We have no plans to keep him away from her, but he won't be living with her anymore.

"Momma, can we make cookies after school?" Sophia asks from the backseat as we make our way to the Elementary school. As usual, we're running a little behind which seems to be the norm for us these days.

"Yeah. We can do that. What kind do you guys want to make?"

AJ and Sophia spend the next few minutes while we're in the school's drop-off line, debating what kind of treat we should make when I pick them up later.

"Love you, Momma," Sophia shouts just as AJ calls out, "Love you, Momma B." I sit there for a second; speechless and completely stunned. That's the first time AJ has told me that he loved me.

I feel the tears gathering in my eyes as I start to get emotional. Just as I feel a good crying jag coming on, the car behind me lays on the horn and breaks the moment. I wave my hand in the air and pull back into traffic with a smile on my face. All three of my kids are happy and loved, and I have the most amazing husband to share this adventure with. What more could a woman ask for?

EPILOGUE

Bella

THREE YEARS LATER

"Want you to rest, babe. Sit back and kick your feet up and I'll get lunch taken care of," D tells me, placing a kiss on my head before making his way back over to the grill his dad is watching over.

I hadn't been feeling well for the last two weeks and thought that I had picked up a stomach bug from work. Diesel, having had enough of me feeling unwell, insisted I make a doctor's appointment and even took off from work to go with me. To say that it shocked us to learn that we were pregnant is the understatement of the century. Of course, my husband is thrilled about adding another child to our brood.

Since finding out that I'm going to have a baby, he's been hovering more than usual and doting on me at every turn. I've never had anyone take care of me the way my husband does. It's an incredible feeling to be loved the way D loves me and our kids.

"Paige, how are things going at the new office? It's a bigger space than before, isn't it?"

"We are loving it and yes, it's about twice the size of our last building and definitely bigger than working out of that small office at King Crow Ink. We had to hire a new receptionist since the last one was stolen," she says not upset about the loss in the slightest. "We are also thinking about bringing in another attorney. I'm not sure what my husband is going to think about us bringing in a man, though. Although, he doesn't mind that I work closely with Shane all day long. Probably helps we bat for the same team, though," she says, laughing about her husband's territorial nature.

"Daddy, look," Luke yells from the swing, as he tries to go as high as Sophia.

"I see buddy. You're going to be as high as Sis before you know it." The relationship between Lucas and Diesel is what you would imagine a father and son would be. Trevor is missing out but Luke doesn't have a clue what it's like to be without a father figure because Diesel stepped into the role from day one. In the last three years, Trevor hasn't learned from his mistakes and I honestly don't think he even cares anymore that Luke has more of a bond with D than anyone else. Not that it would matter what he thinks anyway.

"Babe, you guys want to clear off that table? The food is just about ready," D shouts.

Paige and I quickly clear away the toys as D sets the platter of burgers on the patio table. Hearing that the food is ready, the kids come running. They've been hollering that they're hungry for the last twenty minutes, so I didn't expect they'd waste any time.

Once everyone is situated with a plate in front of them, D looks at me with a raised brow in question. He is dying to announce that we're expecting. I give him a subtle nod, and he grins back at me. Wrapping his arm around my shoulders, he clears his throat to get everyone's attention. As soon as he has it, he says, "Bella and I have some news that we want to share with all of you. In eight and a half months, we'll be welcoming a new member into our family."

"Are we getting a dog?" Sophia shouts excitedly making us all laugh.

"No princess, we're having a baby. Your momma has a baby growing in her belly," D tells her.

"Aww man. Can we get a dog too?" Luke asks. He's the one who started all the dog talk a few weeks ago.

"I hope it's a boy," AJ shouts over the noise of everyone talking at once. His comment leads to the debate of girls versus boys. As I sit back and watch my family fuss over the gender of the baby growing in my belly, I know without a doubt I'm so blessed to have this amazing family.

"Make me a son, babe. It's hard enough with the two beauties I have already. Keeping boys away from another girl that will no doubt be as beautiful as her momma and sister will be impossible," D laughs, jumping right back into the fray of boys vs. girls.

I'm so thankful for the day I met Diesel in the parking lot of King Crow Ink and that the love we share is unshakable and runs soul deep.

The End... For Now

!! THANK YOU !!

THANK YOU!!!

Thank you for taking the time to read Diesel and Bella's story. I hope you enjoyed following them through their journey as they found their happily ever after.

If you want to know what happens with the rest of the King Crow Ink Crew, stay tuned as these sexy ink slingers find the ladies that are sure to bring them to their knees.

ALSO BY MADALYN JUDGE

More books by Madalyn Judge

KING CROW INK

Diesel - Soul Deep (King Crow Ink Book 1)

Layla – Welcome to Miami (King Crow Ink Book 2) TBA

Miami Saints Mc

Vexing Viper OCTOBER 13

Saving Sparrow TBA

ABOUT THE AUTHOR

🩶 About Madalyn Judge 🩶

I write stories about tattoo hotties and badass bikers under the Pen name Madalyn Judge. I live in small town Kentucky and there's nowhere else I'd rather be. I love the slower pace and unbreakable roots that take hold when you live in a place like this. I have traveled from Germany to California, to Georgia, and a lot of other places in between. There's still no place like home.

I'm married to the best man I know and together we have two children that are now grown, adults.

Madalyn Judge is the braver part of me and I would have never had the courage to write and publish my own stories without her. I had been toying with the idea of writing a book, and it took getting schooled by my youngest child for me to just go for it. There is nothing quite like having your words thrown back at you by your children. When you tell them they can do anything they set their minds to and that the only thing that can ever hold them back is themselves. Well, you have to live up to that when they come back at you.

So, I decided to let all the stories and characters that had been rattling around in my brain out into the world.

Follow Me on Social Media by clicking the icons below.

UNTITLED

STAY CONNECTED

Check out Madalyn's website and sign up for our newsletter, so you're notified every time a new book is released.
    MADALYNJUDGEBOOKS.COM

Printed in Great Britain
by Amazon